"Aren't you ashamed of what you're doing?"

"*Me?* Ashamed?" Hester marveled at his lack of understanding. "It's my mother who's ashamed. If you had a come-by-chance child, you'd take a bit of interest in it, wouldn't you?"

"I do!" Demetrios looked into her shocked eyes. "That's part of my proposition. I'm offering you a life free from monetary worries together with the twenty thousand pounds you're demanding, but in return I expect to get a stepmother for my own daughter."

"And what makes you think I'd even consider—"

"Simple," he interrupted her. "I don't give you much for your chances with Vilma." Demetrios leaned back in his chair and surveyed her blandly. "And I shall expect you to give me a son."

There wasn't all that much to think about....

These books may be available at your local bookseller.

Don't miss any of our special offers. Write to us at the following address for information on our newest releases.

Harlequin Reader Service
P.O. Box 52040, Phoenix, AZ 85072-2040
Canadian address: P.O. Box 2800, Postal Station A,
5170 Yonge St., Willowdale, Ont. M2N 6J3

JENETH MURREY

the daughter of night

Harlequin Books

TORONTO • NEW YORK • LONDON
AMSTERDAM • PARIS • SYDNEY • HAMBURG
STOCKHOLM • ATHENS • TOKYO • MILAN

Harlequin Presents first edition May 1985
ISBN 0-373-10787-0

Original hardcover edition published in 1983
by Mills & Boon Limited

CHAPTER ONE

OVER the noise of the hissing water of the shower and the patter of it as it fell into the tiled basin, Hester heard the ring of the doorbell and tried to ignore it. If it was a friend or an acquaintance, there would be three rings and then silence because, if she didn't answer, whoever it was would either drop a note through the letterbox or go away and come back later. That was the code she had with people she knew—just three rings.

She turned on the taps a little more so that the needle jets became fierce and stung the skin of her back as she stood luxuriating. She'd had a busy day and this was a good and pleasant way of getting some life back into her tired body—but the bell continued to ring, and no longer in short bursts. It was now a continuous, high-pitched buzz which demanded attention, something nobody could ignore.

Whoever was outside the door must be leaning on the button, it was a stiff little bell push and a single finger would have become tired long before now. Reluctantly, Hester switched off the shower and considered what to do. She couldn't let the ringing go on and on, the batteries in the bell would run down and she had no spares, so the bell wouldn't work in the morning when her neighbour, a hardworking secretary, gave her the usual call at seven.

Her normally soft mouth thinned to a hard line as she stepped out of the shower, rubbed herself roughly dry and struggled her still damp body into a towelling robe, and there was a fighting gleam in her brown eyes as, halfway across her living room, she caught sight of herself in the mirror. With a vexed scowl she tightened the sash of the robe more securely and pulled off the bulky shower cap, shaking her hair loose so that it fell about her shoulders.

It was good, thick hair, the shade of old mahogany with a natural wave which made it easy to style—just the sort of hair a hairdresser needed—an advertisement for any salon, and the salon for which she worked was very high class. Within its hallowed and expensive portals, each assistant had been chosen not only for qualifications and ability but also for hair quality and the correct deferential approach.

She pattered on bare feet down the mini-hallway and yelled, 'Who's there?' as her fingers struggled with the lock of the door.

There wasn't any answer to her demand, the bell went on ringing and nothing, it seemed, would stop it until she opened the door and gave whoever was there a piece of her mind. Not only was she being disturbed, but so were all the other tenants on the floor, and she'd get a nasty look from her landlady in the morning.

'Can't you take a hint?' she demanded angrily as at last her still wet fingers managed to turn the knob of the Yale lock. She opened the door a few inches and held it there while her other hand reached for the safety chain to push it into the slot—but she didn't get that opportunity. The man outside raised his shoulder from where it had been leaning on the bell push and put a hand on the door, shoving it inwards so that the chain and its little brass knob dangled impotently, several inches too short to bridge the gap.

'Miss Hester Marsh?'

She leaned all her weight against the door and

glared at him through the narrow gap. The man was a complete stranger, and her nostrils thinned with temper.

'Whatever you're selling, I don't want any!'

'I'm not selling.'

'You aren't?' she snapped it off sharply. 'Then go away and don't bother me. I'm not interested in opinion polls, and market research leaves me cold. Go and bother somebody else!'

'They don't interest me either.' The man continued to push against the door, forcing it open against her restraining hand and body as though he had some God-given right to intrude where he wasn't wanted. 'I want to talk to you, and I'd prefer to do that in private.'

Hester's patience, never very long-suffering except with the clientele of the salon, snapped—rage welled up in her, drowning the little fear which had been growing at his attempts to force the door against her.

'You can't come in here.' She pushed back with all her might. 'I don't care what you want, you don't force your way in here, not without an invitation, and if you're the police, show me your warrant card.'

'So you're expecting the police.' He sounded satisfied.

'You're not one of them,' she panted as she struggled to prevent the door opening any further. 'Your manners aren't good enough. I advise you to go before I start screaming!'

The pressure against her increased, the bottom of the door caught against her bare foot and she yelped with pain, jumping backwards quickly—and then the man was inside, pushing her away and closing the door firmly behind him.

'Start screaming,' he advised nastily. 'If somebody

is stupid enough to come to your rescue, I shall simply tell them I'm here at your invitation.'

'Oh, very clever!' Hester grabbed at errant folds of her towelling wrap, and retied the sash, belting it more firmly about her. Then she drew herself upright, took a deep breath and regained a little of the dignity she had lost in her humiliating struggle. The man had bested her, he was inside, and her impotent rage was giving way to a nameless fear.

'Since you're already in,' she spat, 'perhaps you'll explain just why you're forcing yourself on me!' She crushed the fear down under a chilly exterior and faced him defiantly.

'I told you—I want to talk to you, it's as simple as that.' She thought she detected a very faint foreign intonation in his voice but couldn't be sure, and she wrinkled her eyebrows in puzzlement. 'I'm not going to attack you,' he continued smoothly.

No—her glance flickered over him—this man wouldn't need to attack a woman. At a guess, she thought he could probably have any girl he fancied. Things about him started to register with her. He was far too well dressed to be any sort of a salesman—her eyes appreciated the quality and cut of his clothes. There was solid value there—a conservative value— nothing out of the way or even ultra-fashionable. She judged him to be well off and used to giving orders— used to having his own way.

All the same—her nose wrinkled like a cat which smelled danger—here he was, a complete stranger, an intruder, yet he knew her name and where she lived. She couldn't place him in the scheme of things.

'Were you expecting the police?' He repeated the question.

'Are you out of your mind?' Hester gave a snort of

exasperation. She disliked mysteries. 'Since you're this far in, you'd better come the whole way. The light's better in my living room and I want to be able to describe you properly when I file a complaint. As for the police, I should think you've a damn sight more reason to be scared of them than I have—I don't force my way in where I'm not wanted,' and with a shrug, she turned and led the way into the bedsitting room. 'And your explanation had better be a good one,' she snapped, 'or I *will* make a complaint.'

'Oh, I don't think you'll do that.' He was imperturbable and he stood quietly, making her cosy room look somehow small and tawdry. 'But if you did, you'd need my name. It's Demetrios Thalassis. Does that ring a bell?'

'It tolls a knell!' she corrected him. 'Did Vilma—my mother send you?' And she caught the gleam of very white, very even teeth as his mouth curved into a half-moon smile. Now she could place him, and the faint trace of accent. Greek, like Vilma's husband.

'Nobody sends me anywhere, my dear Hester,' he murmured. 'Vilma came to me—she was in trouble, money trouble, and she told me all about it. I don't like members of my family being blackmailed.' He reached into his pocket and came out with a cigarette case. Hester's eyes noted the gleam of gold and the deeply cut monogram before he produced a matching lighter, lit a cigarette and restored his valuables to his pocket.

'So,' he continued smoothly, 'I came to see for myself. And speaking of the police, I suppose you're aware you face an extremely serious charge—demanding money with menaces?'

'Do smoke, if you want to,' Hester said wearily, wondering if this was her mother's idea of a bully boy or had they some other sort of relationship. 'Have you brought the money?'

'Do I look that mad?' Without asking, he hitched a chair towards him with his foot and sat down as though he owned the place.

'And please make yourself comfortable.' Her eyes narrowed, glittering between their thick fringes of lashes. 'If you haven't brought the money, why have you come at all?'

'To size up the opposition, of course.' He blew a perfect smoke ring, his very dark eyes never leaving her face. 'In the course of my life, I've encountered villains of all shapes and sizes, but this is the first time I've ever met a female blackmailer. I was curious about you before, and now I've met you, I'm even more curious. You aren't what I expected.'

'There's a pattern for female blackmailers?' Hester was beginning to find her feet and she had decided that any show of fear would be taken as weakness. Instead, she raised a cool eyebrow. 'You must really tell me what it is so that I can dress the part next time.'

'You certainly don't look like a girl with criminal tendencies.' His eyes slid over her from the crown of her head to the soles of her bare feet. 'Given the right clothes and a short course in mannerly behaviour. . . .'

'Mannerly behaviour!' Her voice rose indignantly. 'Look who's talking about manners—forcing your way into my flat. . . .'

'. . . As I said,' he interrupted her interruption without blinking an eyelid, 'some good clothes and a few lessons in behaviour and you could be quite something. Is that why you want Vilma to give you twenty thousand pounds? But tell me, please, why do you think she *should* give it to you?'

Hester smiled at him wolfishly. She had ignored the bit about clothes but the remark about her manners had hit hard and to cover it, she became crude.

'Oh lord! Vilma's picked herself a right one this time, but you can't be her husband, although you do have the same name—she wouldn't have told him about this—not about me, so I suppose you're some sort of minor relation. A very minor one, I'd guess—a little dog she's sent out to bark for her.'

'And I bite as well.'

'You may bite,' she pointed out curtly, 'but you haven't brought the money!'

'And you're a very cool customer.' He blew another smoke ring. 'Are your demands always so blunt, and don't you ever worry about prosecution?'

'Oh,' she gestured largely, 'it's my first try at the business—you can't expect a professional approach, not at this stage, and as for prosecution, why should I worry about that? I didn't put anything in writing and there weren't any witnesses. It was all strictly between Vilma and me—until you butted in,' she added angrily.

'And you don't count me as a witness?'

'No,' she gave him a tight smile with no mirth in it. 'Remember, I didn't ask you for money, merely whether you'd brought it. As you haven't, you've made a needless journey, so you'd better run back to Vilma and tell her she's pushing it. The deadline's the end of this week, which gives her just four clear days. After that, the balloon goes up!'

'And the penalty if she doesn't meet your deadline?'

Hester's mirthless grin widened almost as though she could savour triumph. 'I have a friend who's in the newspaper business. He works for a rather pink publication, a widely read weekly, and he's dedicated himself to printing the lowdown on those who live the high life. He loves his work—I suppose you could call him a compulsive stirrer up of mud and I should imagine that after his first instalment on the present Mrs Sandros Thalassis, her husband, reported as being a strict and devoted family man, will retire to a lonely villa somewhere with egg on his face.'

'Your friend's going to write all this in four days?' Demetrios Thalassis ground out his half smoked cigarette.

Hester laughed in his face. 'What do you take me for—a fool? No, the first instalment's nearly ready, but the bit I can add is a bombshell—it's such a well kept secret, not common knowledge like the rest. That'll make it that much spicier, don't you think, and Vilma won't have an invitation to the next Garden Party. In fact, I think some of her high-placed friends will cool off rapidly.'

'I was wrong about you.' He remained calm, but there were white patches of temper at the corners of his nostrils, though the emotion was controlled perfectly; his voice was still calm and almost lazy. 'I thought you were a young girl who'd been led astray, who wanted her name in the papers, but you're more than that, you're a bitch of the first water.'

'So I'm a bitch!' she flared. 'Who cares? I don't, it doesn't worry me. I want that money and Vilma can afford it. It's not as if I was mugging an O.A.P. for the few coins in her purse. If Vilma's reluctant to have her husband know—if she can't raise the cash—you can tell her to sell a few of those diamonds she wears to parties. Just as long as it adds up to twenty thousand pounds!'

'Which is rather a large sum to keep you quiet about a piffling little indiscretion which took place when she was very young.' Demetrios Thalassis' face was a mask of distaste, and Hester watched him warily as she estimated the strength of the opposition.

He wasn't as tall as she'd first thought, slightly under six foot, but his breadth of shoulder had misled her—powerfully built men often looked bigger than they really were. He was also extremely good-looking—his black, glossy hair clung in short curls to a well shaped skull—his eyes were large and well spaced, although half their beauty was hidden by long, curling, almost feminine lashes and the heavy eyelids. His nose, she decided, was arrogant and his mouth had a sensual curve that sent a small shiver down her spine but at his chin, she stopped. It was like granite—this wasn't a man she wanted to tangle with, but she had no choice, apparently, and she wasn't giving up now or being frightened off, there was too much at stake.

She tried to imagine the scene between him and Vilma—Vilma, small, blonde, looking far younger than her years and weeping softly all over that wide chest—but not so much as to damage her make-up or make her mascara run. Maybe she had confessed to a tiny indiscretion—almost nothing really—Hester could almost hear the words dropping reluctantly, interspersed with tiny sobs. 'It had all happened so many, many years ago'—when Vilma was little more than a child.

Hester's thoughts took another direction. This man, whoever he was—whatever the connection between him and Vilma—he wasn't a nobody. Vilma would never waste her time buttering up a mere nonentity. She felt her temper slipping from the hard control she was putting on it and she made no further attempt to keep it in check.

'A little indiscretion!' She almost shouted it at him.

'Do I look that "little"? Yes,' as she saw his mouth tighten, the sensual curve straightening out into a hard, straight line, 'don't tell me Vilma's only given you half a tale, and don't look so surprised. I'm five foot five inches, and that's rather large to be called a "little indiscretion" any longer!'

'You're implying that you're Vilma's daughter?'

Hester steeled herself to speak normally and not yell 'Yes!' in his face. She waved a hand airily instead. 'You don't catch on very quickly, do you?' She made it sound as sarcastic as possible and gave it a smile to match. 'Or has my mother been telling lies about her age again? The last quote in the gossip columns put her at thirty-eight, although she prefers to say thirty-six. Since you're part of her new husband's family and not exactly blind, I would have thought you'd know that was an understatement. Her little indiscretion took place all of twenty-five years ago and she was well over the age of consent at the time. I'm twenty-four and a bit—work it out for yourself!'

'It could have been rape,' he suggested mildly.

'It was!' she retorted, 'but not the way you think, not the way you hope. When I'd traced my mother, I went down to the little place where she'd been living at the time—very small and everybody knows everybody. Apparently I'm very like my father, so I hardly had to ask—I was directed to where his mother was living by at least four very helpful people in the local pub.' She paused, the grimness of her face softened by sorrow and a faint, wry pity.

'He was dead, of course. He'd gone out to Australia, worked on sheep stations and with rodeos—that was where he was killed—and they'd sent his few personal effects back to his mother since he had no other relatives. She showed them to me and in the box was a little bundle of notes and letters, all tied up with pink ribbon. The poor, romantic fool, he'd actually loved her! Anyway, those notes and things proved who'd raped whom!'

'But if Vilma's your mother, as you say. . . .'

'I don't just say it, I can prove it, so there's no "if" about it,' Hester interrupted him swiftly and fiercely. 'My dear little mother covered it all up very successfully. She'd left things too late for an abortion, so she went on a "six-month cruise" to explain her absence from the social scene. Everything was very neat and tidy and nobody would ever have known if the law hadn't been changed and I was allowed to trace her as soon as I was old enough. She gave me away the day I was born in the place where she'd spent the last few weeks of her "cruise", and she didn't even bother about a reputable adoption agency—I suppose she thought that might be traced. Oh no, I went into a Council orphanage as an abandoned baby.'

During the last part of this, she had turned her back on him to look out of the window at the gathering shadows of the spring evening and to hide the hurt which she knew must be showing on her face, but now she swung round on him like a tiger. 'She didn't tell anybody, not even my father's mother who would have been quite willing to bring me up. The old lady's dead now, so that part of it doesn't matter any more. You're looking at me as though I was dirt, aren't you? Well, I am! I'm Vilma's dirt which she carefully swept under the carpet—something to be forgotten, ignored and as quickly as possible—but I won't be forgotten! Now, you get back to her and tell her she has until the end of this week to pay up. I traced her as soon as it was possible and I was able—it took a bit of time and a lot of money which I could ill afford, but I did it, and now I've got my birth certificate to prove what I say and,' she smiled tightly into his rigid face, 'you can tell her, while you're about it, that I can put a name to that blank space she left in the column marked "Father". That should make her all the more eager to have the whole thing kept quiet!'

Demetrios Thalassis moved slightly in his chair, although he continued to look enigmatic. 'This makes you one of the family,' he murmured.

'Thank you for nothing!' She spat it at him. 'Vilma's kind of family is something I can do without.'

He frowned her into silence. 'I'm speaking about the Thalassis family, so kindly be silent while I work this out. We apparently owe you something. . . .'

'You—*your* family owes me nothing,' she broke in on him stormily. 'It's Vilma who owes me and it's Vilma who's going to pay. She can afford it, this is her second wealthy husband and she has money of her own anyway. Tell her to spare some of that!'

'And if you get the money?' He raised eyebrows, black and arched. 'What do you intend doing with it?'

'When, not if,' she corrected him. 'And it's none of your business what I do with it. Personally, I'd like to burn the whole lot under her nose, but I've got a better use for it. Now, if you'll please go—it's not midsummer and I'm getting cold.' She smoothed out her voice to a polite flatness, all trace of anger and any other emotion wiped away. 'Thank you for calling, Mr Thalassis, although I can't say I've enjoyed meeting you or that your visit has given me very much pleasure. . . .'

'Not yet,' he made no attempt to rise. 'I'm thinking about your future, I don't want this sort of thing happening again, and twenty thousand pounds isn't very much by today's standards. . . .'

'Now, that's a change in your tune,' she marvelled brightly. 'A few minutes ago you called it "rather a large sum". What's happened to make you change your mind?'

He shrugged, ignoring her as though she hadn't spoken. 'Do you intend to invest it—maybe start up a business of your own, or have you some idea of marriage? It wouldn't even buy you a decent house.'

'And as I said before,' Hester stood very erect and looked down on him haughtily, 'it's none of your business what I do, but, just for the record, I've a very good job and no intention of changing it—also, I've no intention of getting married. In my layer of society, that's not quite the ideal state as pictured in the glossy magazines. Ordinary housewives are expected to cook and clean—stay at home and look after babies. No, thank you, that's not my idea of life!'

'Then perhaps a new wardrobe and a year to catch a wealthy husband . . .?'

'That does it!' Almost without thinking, her rage was so great, she had grasped his shoulder and was pulling him from the chair, anger lending strength to her hands. 'You can speculate all you want on the way back to where you came from. As I said, it's no concern of yours. So just go back to Vilma and tell her she hasn't much time left.'

He shook off her hands as though there was no particle of strength in her grip. 'Don't tell me what to do, Miss Hester Marsh! I'm merely considering if and how you should be paid. If I decide you should have the money, I then have to work out how best to pay you. . . .'

'Cash,' she answered promptly. 'No cheques, I don't want anything traceable. What is it they say in the movies?—small denomination notes and in a paper bag—I want to be able to count it! Knowing Vilma, and you do get to know a person when you've spent the best part of your adult life tracing them—she's quite likely to try short-changing me. Money sticks to her little fingers like glue—she can't bear to part with it. And I don't want money from your family, that would spoil the whole thing—it'll hurt her that much more to have to part with her own.' She took a deep breath. 'Now you can call me a bitch, I deserve it!' And without waiting for a reply, she stormed into the tiny bathroom, slammed the door viciously, locked it and began to dress her shivering body in the clothes laid out ready.

Her teeth were chattering as she wriggled her chilled body into bra, panties and tights, topped them with the towelling robe which was still damp so that she shivered even more, and then waited for the sound of movement in the bedsitting room. She had no intention of leaving her refuge until he was gone.

It seemed like an age before she heard his footsteps leaving the room and going down the mini-hallway, and then came the sound of the quiet closing of her door onto the landing. She had taken off her watch before she showered and it was still lying where she'd left it on the mantelpiece in her bedsitting room, so she had no means of telling the time, so she sat on the stool beside the shower cabinet and counted slowly up to two hundred. After that, she took the catch off the bathroom door, opened it and poked her head round the narrow gap, still listening. She wasn't going to be caught again—she'd heard of people who slammed a door and then hid behind it, but everything was silent and there was that indefinable feeling that the flat was empty, so she felt it safe to emerge from her hiding place.

Picking up her watch, she gazed at the clear little face

as though she could hardly believe so little time had passed since Demetrios Thalassis had forced his way into her bedsitter flat. She felt as exhausted as if she had been battling verbally with him for hours and hours, and reaction was setting in so that her slender body shook with tremors of cold and exhaustion. Wearily, she lit the middle bar of the gas fire, went into the microscopic kitchenette and started to make a pot of tea.

Her mouth was dry and her head was beginning to ache, so, while the kettle was boiling, she hunted through her bag for a couple of aspirins and, at last, sat down on the rug before the fire with her tea, to stare wearily at the glowing element, paying no attention to the hisses and whistling pops which the fire emitted. It always did that. Now she had to think.

Quietly she went over in her mind the contents of her bedsit. There was nothing here that could give him a lead, of that she was sure. Here she was Hester Marsh who lived alone, there were no traces of her past life, nothing which would lead anywhere but to this rather dreary little place. That was good; she didn't want anybody else involved. Her musings were interrupted by a ring on the doorbell and for a moment every muscle in her body tightened in fear that it might be him again, come back to torment her some more, but there was a second ring and a third, which meant it was safe, and she scrambled to her feet to go and open the door.

It was only her landlady, who could be garrulous at times, and evidently this was going to be one of them.

'Everything all right, Miss Marsh?' The woman's face was filled with curiosity. 'I didn't know whether I should let your visitor up, but he seemed to know you—had your name off pat and he looked quite respectable. . . .'

'Quite all right,' Hester manufactured a smile. 'But his visit delayed me a bit,' she indicated her robe. 'I was just going to take a shower when he arrived.'

'Looked like one of those lawyer fellows.' The landlady seemed determined to learn as much as she could and Hester knew from experience that she would ask questions until she had some sort of tale that satisfied her.

'Mmm,' she nodded, and smiled again. 'A small bequest, nothing much, not even worth a visit to his office, but you know how these legal people are, they have to satisfy themselves that I am who I am even if it's only a matter of a few pounds. And now,' she started to close the door, 'if you'll excuse me, I've got a date tonight and I'm late already.'

The landlady went off downstairs with sufficient misinformation to keep her happy for the rest of the week, and Hester closed the door and went back to the fire, slumping down on the rug and feeling sorry for herself.

Trust Vilma to make things as awkward as possible! It would have been so simple for her to pay up and keep quiet, but as Hester had told Demetrios Thalassis, Vilma wasn't like that. She'd got away with so many things in her life, she was greedy and couldn't bear to part with a penny, so Hester might have known she'd try to frighten her daughter off and she'd nearly succeeded.

But Hester was convinced that everything would be all right now. Tonight, she'd been taken by surprise; she had been expecting quite a battle with Vilma, but she hadn't allowed for having to fight that battle with an unknown quantity like Demetrios Thalassis. Even so, she grinned weakly to herself, she hadn't done so badly. In any other circumstances, Flo would have been proud of her!

Flo! Hester stared into the fire, remembering her foster-mother. Dear Flo, warm, kind and loving, with a maternal complex as big as the dome of St Paul's. Flo, who could never have a child of her own because of a rhesus negative blood factor, and Hester had always thought herself to be Flo's child. She'd known all about Mia, Flo's orphaned niece who had been adopted and come to live with them when she, Hester, had been five, but herself she had always thought of as really belonging.

It wasn't until she was eighteen that Flo had explained about her own fostering, and Hester had been angry at the thought of another, unknown mother. She could remember the scene as though it had only happened yesterday—herself being angry and hurt and Flo, stern and just but loving and understanding.

'She's *not* my mother,' Hester had stormed. 'She gave me away. I don't want to know anything about her!' and Flo had interrupted.

'Don't you speak like that, my girl. There's lots of reasons why your mother could have given you away. Women don't do that without cause, not to their own babies. Maybe she's been grieving all these years, but now you've got the chance to set her mind at rest. So stop getting into one of your paddys! Your dad and I loved you both, neither one more than the other, for all Mia's my brother's child. We chose you, remember, and your dad would turn in his grave if he could hear you now!'

'I'm sorry.' Hester had brushed away her tears with the back of her hand and allowed a watery smile to peep through. 'But I've always thought of myself as your daughter. It's been a bit of a blow.'

'And you're still my girl,' Flo had been brisk. 'Nothing will ever change that.'

Hester had been partly mollified, but only partly. 'I still don't want to know anything about her.' She had been flatly positive, and at that time she had meant every word, but that was before Flo became so very ill—a blood disease, all to do with that rhesus negative factor—and Mia, now a staff nurse, had found a Swiss specialist who had offered some hope.

It had cost nearly the earth to see the man when he paid a visit to London and then his prognosis had been overly cautious, but so very much more hopeful than that of any other doctor Flo had been to. If he could have Flo in his Swiss clinic for six months, although a year might be better. . . .

'He might as well ask us to send her to the moon!' Mia had been heartbroken. 'We could maybe afford the fare to get her there, but did you hear what it would cost to keep her there—five hundred pounds a week! We just haven't got that kind of money.'

It was at that moment that Hester had her bright idea. She, despite her protest, had already done a bit of work in tracing her own mother. She had at least established that she was a wealthy woman, and Hester reckoned that her mother owed Flo this much at least. A little further investigation had proved to her that Flo was owed much more than that. She had concocted her plot and then discussed it with Mia, who wasn't enthusiastic, but Mia had always been a scaredy-cat and rather timid.

'As long as Flo doesn't know,' she had said, 'and as long as you don't get yourself into trouble. . . .'

Hester had qualms herself, but she put a brave face on it. 'Poh! I'm not doing anything illegal, I'm just asking my own mother to give me some money—that's quite within the law, isn't it?' And at Mia's nod, she had gone off to her bedsit to put her plan into operation.

Of course, she hadn't been able to tell Mia the whole of it and they hadn't told Flo any part. Doing either of those things would have doomed it from the start. Flo was rigidly honest, she wouldn't have accepted a penny from anybody else, and Mia was too timid. She would have balked at blackmail and given the whole thing away in no time flat.

CHAPTER TWO

HALF an hour later, dressed in a lovat tweed skirt, a matching sweater, a suede jacket and soft casual shoes, Hester left her flatlet to visit Mia and Flo. She had originally intended to take a taxi, but something inside her was being very cautious. She had tried laughing it off, jeering at herself for suspecting that Demetrios Thalassis would have her followed, something out of a second-rate T.V. thriller, she told herself—it wouldn't happen to her, but caution won. There was too much at stake—Flo's health, maybe even her life—for Hester to be careless.

Instead she went by tube from Finsbury Park to Holborn, where she changed for Mile End, and once there, she threaded her way through streets which were as familiar to her as the back of her own hand— she could have walked them blindfold to find the block of Council flats which had been all the home she'd ever known until a few years ago. Several people— acquaintances from her youth—hailed her and stopped to speak, giving messages for Flo and admiring the flowers she was carrying, and she answered them and their questions cheerily, knowing it wasn't just curiosity which prompted them but real interest. Flo was a neighbour and a good neighbour in this tight-knit community of East Enders.

She avoided the lift—too many times she'd found it broken down—and made straight for the stairs, nearly running up all four flights of them to arrive at the flat door out of breath. She was nearly an hour late. There was no need to knock, she still had a key, and she went into the parlour softly.

'How is she?' Hester kept her voice down and Mia, who was stripping off her nurse's uniform, turned to her with a glad smile.

'No worse today.' Mia spoke in little more than a whisper. Flo had keen ears and the walls were far from soundproof. 'Did you get it?'

Hester made a little face to indicate her lack of success so far. 'But I shall, Mia—don't worry so.'

Mia fluffed up her light brown hair which the cap had flattened and her glad smile turned to an expression of doom. 'But I do worry, Hes. I worry about you and what you're doing all the time. You're going to get yourself into trouble, I know you are. It was a mad idea!'

'More desperate than mad, I'd say,' Hester grinned. 'But desperate affairs need desperate remedies, and as I've always pointed out, I'm not doing anything illegal.'

'I know all that,' Mia still looked worried, 'you've told me before. There's nothing wrong with a girl asking her own mother for some money to tide her over a bad patch—that's what you say, but it can't be as easy as that! It's an awful lot of money,' she finished gloomily.

'It's what we need.' Hester was bracing while managing to convey a feeling of tranquil certainty.

'And you're sure you haven't said anything about wanting it for her?' Mia's head nodded to indicate the bedroom next door. 'She wouldn't like it, you know, in fact she'd get straight out of that bed and bat your ears.' She gave a weak chuckle of laughter. 'She's done it before. . . .' And then she sobered. 'Damn everything, nothing's fair in this world! Why should she have to put up with this when there are millions of women who get away with murder and never have to suffer a day? She's never done a bad thing in her life, and then this has to happen to her!'

'You're still glooming, so stop it,' Hester ordered. 'I've told you, it's going to be all right. I'll go in and see her now—is she expecting me?'

'Been waiting all day for just this moment.' Mia looked wry. 'Isn't it funny—I'm her real relation, proper family, and yet I can't cope with her as well as you can. I don't seem to be able to give her any comfort.'

'Which is why I left to live on my own.' Hester slipped an arm around her foster-sister's narrow shoulders. 'I've told you all this before, so why do you keep harping on it? Flo loves us both, but I thought she ought to love you just that little bit more. You never had a chance, you poor kid, I always made far too much noise and got myself into too many scrapes. I was demanding attention, of course. I must have been a right little horror.'

'You were nothing of the kind!' Mia was indignant and then she smiled reminiscently. 'Remember how you used to slap the boys who pulled my hair?'

'Vividly,' Hester chuckled. 'I've a shrewd suspicion I always liked chucking my weight about—the number of times Flo's tanned me, but it never did much good—and speaking of Flo, shall I go in and see her now?'

'She'll be crawling out here on her hands and knees if you don't,' Mia smiled ruefully. 'Your coming is the high spot of her day except when the woman across the way comes in to feed the plants. They have a right old natter.'

Flo Marsh was sitting up in bed, supported by a

great many pillows—a small, sparrowlike woman, pale and almost bloodless, but her eyes were bright and sharp, they softened when she looked at Hester.

'Oh, you shouldn't have, you bad girl, wasting your money like this!' but she seized on the flowers and buried her nose in the blossoms. The sleeves of her bedjacket fell back to disclose thin, sticklike arms and her hands were no more than skin and bone. 'You're late,' she said severely.

Hester's heart squeezed painfully, but she knew better than to mention Flo's illness—that wasn't allowed. 'You've had Mia to bully in the interval, so what are you complaining about?' She sat down on the side of the bed and produced a box of sweets. 'Don't tell Mia, she'll confiscate them to stop you from getting fat. As a matter of fact, I was delayed by a man—he just wouldn't let me get away from him,' she teased. 'I was tempted to give him a bit of encouragement, what do you think? After all, I'm getting on. . . .'

'Don't talk such nonsense!' Her foster-mother gazed at her fondly. 'And like I've told you before, you want to be careful, especially if he looks well-to-do and with a car and all. There's too many of that sort hanging about and they've an eye for the girls. Trouble for you, but they think nothing of it—it's a bit of fun for them. He's not like that, I hope.'

'Not a bit,' Hester chuckled. 'He looked like being the persistent type, but I think I made a bad impression on him.' She delved into her capacious shoulder-bag and extracted a bloodthirsty-looking paperback, the sort that her foster-mother adored, and stayed talking for another hour, until at last they came to Mia.

'I've told her,' Flo was vehement, 'there's no need

for her to stay with me all the time—'tisn't good for her. She ought to be out and about, enjoying herself. There's that woman in the flat opposite, she'll come and stay with me in the evenings any time, she said so. You talk to Mia, Hester.'

'And a lot of good that will do,' Hester grimaced. 'You know Mia, you should by now—she's your own niece, and she won't leave you while you're ill. When you're better, we'll all have a holiday together. I'll go and tell her you're ready for your medicine, so goodnight, my love—sleep well, and I'll see you tomorrow evening.'

'Is that medicine doing her any good?' she asked Mia, who was in the kitchen, pouring tea and counting out tablets.

'Not much, but at least she sleeps when she's had it.' Mia was still looking worried. 'Hes, I still don't think you should be doing this, asking for money from a stranger. Flo wouldn't like it a bit, and I have to keep biting my tongue to stop from telling her, she asks so many questions.'

'Bite it a bit longer,' Hester advised. 'When the money comes, she's off to that Swiss clinic and you're going with her, so what's the use of worrying now— it's far too late for that. I reckon my mother owes Flo and I'm going to see she pays if I have to beat every penny out of her!'

'But you could get into trouble.' Mia refused to be comforted. 'If she's as wealthy as you say, she's bound to have a bit of pull and she could easily get you the sack. It's such a lot of money!'

'No more than's needed and not even half what Vilma can afford,' Hester snorted. 'Come on, kid, don't get cold feet now. So long as I get the money, I don't care how many jobs I lose or what sort of a job I wind up in. We've had all this out before, don't let's go through it all again.'

'But it might all be for nothing. . . .'

'Look on the bright side, for heaven's sake,' Hester was astringent. 'Does it matter? If the Swiss man can work a miracle, all well and good. If he can't, Flo will have had the best treatment available, a year in his clinic, which is better than a bed on the National Health, isn't it? She'll have you with her on the journey, which will be a comfort for her, you know how she likes company, so stop making mountains out of molehills. Feed Flo her tablets and then we'll have a cup of tea and a sandwich before I get back to my bedsit.'

Lying in bed that night, Hester worked it all out again in her mind. Some people might think her reasoning warped, but she couldn't see it that way. Flo had fostered her from a small baby—admittedly she'd been paid by the local authorities for doing it, a payment which her real mother wouldn't have received, but no amount of money could compensate for all the love and care she had received from the perky little cockney woman whom she still called 'mum'. There had been good times and bad, money had never been plentiful, but they'd always been happy.

Her lips curved tenderly in the darkness as she remembered Flo's frequent economy drives to pay for a week at Margate, school uniform, a tennis raquet, a hockey stick and, later on, her apprenticeship to hairdressing. She, Hester, had been a big drain on the slender resources of the Marsh family, especially after Flo's husband had died. Things had been really tough then until Flo went back to work as a furrier, managing to combine motherhood and a full-time job so that neither Hester nor Mia had ever been or felt neglected.

And Flo had always been strict, there was nothing even faintly permissive about her. Everything was a definite black or white with no confusing grey areas either in behaviour or morals. 'You know right from wrong,' Flo would say—and that was what was bothering Hester now more than anything else. What she was doing was wrong by Flo's standards and she could only thank God that her own were a little more elastic—that she was less of an idealist than Flo.

So she could look at the situation in a practical way—her foster-mother was owed every penny, in fact, twenty thousand pounds was really a small price to pay to get rid of an unwanted child, a child who could have been an embarrassment. And it hadn't cost Vilma a penny—Hester, the daughter of a woman who was wealthy in her own right and who had increased that wealth by two profitable marriages—Hester hadn't cost her mother a brass farthing so far. For nearly twenty-five years she'd been ignored, probably forgotten by the woman who had brought her into the world so carelessly, but now was the time of reckoning.

Spurred into action by the welter of her thoughts, she switched on her bedside lamp and leapt out of bed. On the table was the letter which her landlady had given her when she came back from Flo's.

'Delivered by hand,' the landlady had almost smirked. 'I thought you'd want it straight away and I stayed up special to give it to you when you came in.'

Hester had nodded her thanks and climbed the stairs, determined to leave the wretched thing unopened until morning—she could guess who it was

from. She had set it aside in case whatever was in it
would disturb her night's rest, but it was disturbing
her even more just by being there unopened.

Maybe it was good news, maybe not, but she knew
she wouldn't sleep until she'd read the contents. Her
fingers trembled a little as she slit open the thick white
envelope and extracted the sheet of equally thick white
paper. The writing was bold, black and decisive, and
she scanned it swiftly. 'Dear Hester'—that was an
impertinence for a start—she hadn't granted him the
right to use her given name!

The letter was quite brief, merely saying that a
further meeting would be to their mutual advantage
and that it would be better if it was conducted on
neutral ground—he had felt at some disadvantage in
her small flat. Had he indeed! He hadn't showed it!—
and he felt sure she would feel at an equal
disadvantage in his office. Instead he suggested a well
known Greek restaurant off Shaftesbury Avenue and
he would call for her at half past seven the following
evening. After that, he remained hers, sincerely,
Demetrios Thalassis.

Hester sniffed. Disadvantage—was that what he
called acting as though he owned the place and hadn't
felt too proud of it! All the same, a public eatery had
its advantages; he could hardly come the heavy among
a crowd of diners—added to which, she thought he
spelled danger for her. She wasn't sure what the
danger was, but she was almost sure it existed.

For a moment, a very brief moment, she felt
inclined to stop the whole affair. She wasn't a criminal
by nature and if it hadn't been for Flo's condition,
which was steadily worsening, Hester would have
given up there and then—but no! She knew now that
she *had* to go on, no matter what the consequences.

Yes, of course she would go on. Her soft mouth hardened as she tucked the sheet of paper back into the envelope. She owed it to Flo. Vilma would try to wriggle out of paying and Demetrios Thalassis would undoubtedly give her mother every assistance in that wriggling, but she, Hester, wouldn't be beaten, not so easily. And tomorrow evening she would be cool and businesslike and not let any appeals to her better nature divert her from her purpose by one iota.

Having arrived at this decision, she went back to bed and slept like a baby.

That evening she dressed with care. Her wardrobe wasn't large and she dismissed the black skirt she usually wore for evenings out. A meal at a restaurant hardly warranted a long skirt, especially in the company of Demetrios Thalassis—she didn't have to charm him, and she wasn't in a particularly charming mood to start with.

She inspected the dress she had chosen, a slim-fitting black sheath with a scooped-out neckline. It was a go-anywhere dress, but it needed livening up, so she made up her face nicely so that her eyes were large and mysterious and added a necklace of near-gold leaves so that at half past seven she was ready, and she took a final look in the mirror to comfort herself and to help dispel the queasiness in her stomach. It was no use denying, even to herself, that she wasn't nervous— All day she'd gone over what she would say and do if he refused her the money, and she had been filled with a bitter envy of her mother who could probably go out to a party secure in the knowledge that there was some man to do her dirty work for her. Hester didn't much care for doing her own dirty work, but it had to be done, and she had no man to fall back on.

She had also primed herself with everything she

knew and could discover about Greeks, but the sum total wasn't comforting. They were family-conscious, the man was always the head of the house and family, the females looked to him for care and protection—it was a patriarchal society—marriages were still arranged in country areas and among the more wealthy.

Therefore Demetrios, whatever his relationship to Vilma's husband, would probably follow the family line and try to protect her—and the Thalassis family was very wealthy, owning hotels in every tourist centre around the Mediterranean. Hester gave a bitter little laugh. In the silence of her room it sounded thin and forced—she'd envisaged fighting Vilma, not a wealthy conglomerate!

Demetrios was dead on time, his buzz on the bell was one long one, and she pulled herself together and went to open the door.

'You're ready!' He seemed surprised and his eyes flicked over her with a gleam of appreciation in their dark depths. The gleam offended her, it made her think of slave markets—as though she was on sale, and she snapped upright, her chin in the air.

'Quite ready, unless you've brought the money—in which case you'll have to wait while I count it.'

'But I wasn't bringing it tonight,' he objected, and she suspected he was laughing at her, not taking her seriously enough—perhaps even delaying things a bit. His next words confirmed her suspicions.

'We're merely going one stage further in our negotiations,' he murmured. 'A quiet dinner, that's all. You'd be surprised how many deals are concluded amicably over a good meal and a bottle of wine. This is your coat?' And he reached for her tweed which was hanging on a peg in the hallway.

His car, parked at the kerb, was an example of

restrained magnificence and Hester swiftly rear-
ranged her ideas about him. This was no mere errand
boy to the Thalassis empire—no very junior executive,
even if he was a doer of jobs which others preferred
to stay out of. His petrol bill for a week would pay her
wages at the salon and leave a lot of spending money
over—and errand boys didn't get issued with Rolls-
Royces on the firm.

It suddenly dawned on her that he must be rather
important in the scheme of things, and she felt the
muscles of her stomach twitch with fear—but she
covered her nervousness with an expressionless face,
although her body wouldn't obey her mind so easily.
It insisted on remaining stiff, try as she would to relax,
and he was quick on the uptake—he sensed her fear.

'Relax!' Once again she caught a thread of humour.
'I'm not going to bite yet. That will come later, when
you refuse my final offer.'

'Big of you!' The words left her mouth with a
delicate, female snarl. 'But do be careful, I might bite
back.'

In the dimness of the car she heard his chuckle and
caught the gleam of his teeth as his lips parted in a
smile. He definitely wasn't taking her seriously, he was
treating her and her demand as one big joke. Her lips
firmed and her eyes hardened—she would show him
she was no joke!

The restaurant was a well known one. Hester had
heard of it but never been there, and she discovered
that it was assumed all the patrons could at least read
Greek. There was very little English on the menu and
she couldn't make head or tail of it, so she handed it
back to Demetrios with a shrug.

'It's all beyond me, double Dutch, but I think I'd
like some of those things on skewers,' she flicked a

glance at an adjoining table. 'People seem to be enjoying them.'

'Souvlaka,' he supplied the name, 'and wine?'

'Water,' she corrected, 'or perhaps lemonade. I'm not negotiating through an alcoholic haze.' She was curt and determined—this man was too sure of himself and he had all the advantages—she should have stipulated an ordinary English restaurant. 'When do we talk business?'

'Any time you wish, but no raised voices, please. I'm quite well known here.'

'Then I think we should start now.' Her mouth was firm and her eyes direct. 'Has Vilma agreed?'

There was a slight pause as he gave the waiter their order and she waited impatiently through it, but when the waiter had gone and they were once more alone, the answer was disappointing.

'What do you think?' He was sardonic. 'You said yourself she hates parting with money. . . .'

'She *has* to,' Hester began stormily, then lowered her voice as she became aware of some curious glances from the adjacent table. 'I don't see that she has any option.' She gave Demetrios a glance of pure hatred across the table. 'I suppose you agree with her—the family sticking together and all that?'

'I think money should be earned,' he gave her partial agreement. 'I don't subscribe to donating to causes, no matter how worthy, not unless they've made some effort to help themselves.'

'Oh, hell!' she muttered under her breath as she made way for the waiter and then gazed down at the plate he had put in front of her. She felt sick with disappointment and the food looked revolting. Automatically, she gathered up her bag and made to rise. 'It seems, Mr Thalassis, you've been wasting my time. I'd better get in touch with my mother straight away, her time's running out.'

'Sit down and don't start losing your temper,' he advised calmly in a low voice, and his hand found her wrist across the table and squeezed it mercilessly. 'Don't make a scene.' His voice was low, but there was a threat in his eyes. 'I haven't said you won't have the money, merely that I think it should be earned and not just given to you because of who you are.'

Hester relaxed and put down her bag. 'I could hardly ask for it if I wasn't who I am,' she pointed out sweetly.

'And of course, I have to make sure that you won't make a habit of demanding money from your—er—natural mother.' He ignored her remark as though she hadn't spoken. 'That's a very important point.'

'You don't have to worry about that,' she interrupted. 'This one big payment guarantees a complete loss of memory on my part.'

'But as I said, money should be earned. Are you willing to work for it?'

This was all a game and Hester decided to treat it as such. She shrugged gracefully and applied herself to succulent pieces of lamb and mushroom. 'Provided the work's not too arduous,' she murmured. 'I have to think of my health. What's your proposition?' she demanded. 'And you'd better make it believable, because I'm not a fool and I shan't fall for a con. There's no way I know of earning that amount of money by the weekend, but if you've come up with a bright idea, I'll consider it. I'm open to suggestions and if it's that good, I might even take it up full-time.'

'You still cling to the time limit?' Hester once more had the feeling she was being a source of amusement to him, that he wasn't taking her seriously enough, and her voice sharpened until it gained almost the strident cockney tones of her childhood.

'Of course, it's the done thing among us blackmailers. What's the use of a nebulous threat? It's not forceful enough.' She became aware of his frown and lowered her voice to a husky murmur. 'I work to a timetable—Mrs X this month, Mrs Y next month. I'm a deep-dyed villainess!'

'You're a very charming liar. . . .'

'. . . . And you're wasting my time,' she interrupted forcefully.

'But aren't you ashamed of what you're doing?'

'*Me*? Ashamed? Now why should I be that?' she marvelled at his lack of understanding. 'If somebody's willing to pay to keep their affairs quiet, it's because they're ashamed, not me! Vilma's afraid she might lose her entrée to the upper circles, and having a lot of money, clothes and all the jewellery she needs doesn't mean a thing unless she can show them off in all the right places and to all the right company—go to Cannes, Nice and Monte Carlo on all the right people's yachts . . . .'

'But the right people, as you call them, also have their little secrets,' he pointed out. 'Nobody's without something to remind them of a mistake they once made.'

'And I know that as well,' she retorted. 'But the right people don't abandon a child as Vilma did. Their little bastards exist, but generally there's some responsibility shown for them. There's money for their clothes and education. If you had a come-bychance child, you'd take a bit of interest in it, wouldn't you?'

'I do!' Demetrios laid down his fork and looked into her shocked eyes. 'That's part of my proposition. I'm

offering a home, a wedding ring, a life free from
monetary worries together with twenty thousand
pounds, the sum you're demanding, but in return I
shall expect to get a stepmother for my own—er—
"adopted" daughter. I've chosen you because you
evidently want the money and I think you might have
an empathy with the child, a common bond of
sympathy, feeling as strongly as you do.' He paused as
though considering what to say next, ignoring Hester's
open mouth and stunned expression.

She recovered quickly. 'Not on!' The surprising
thing was that she believed him, but she played for
time. 'I told you, it has to be Vilma's money. Yours
won't do.'

'Oh, it will be,' he assured her, and his smile wasn't
pleasant. 'You could say that I'm the paymaster of the
company, so Vilma won't get her annual and usual
allowance this year and since she won't be able to
complain to her husband—who, by the way is my
uncle—she'll have to make up the deficit out of her
own pocket, won't she?'

'Her husband allows her twenty thousand pounds a
year?' Hester almost gulped for breath. To her, it was
all the wealth of the Indies, and she couldn't bring
herself to believe that one person could spend that
amount of money in just twelve months.

'No,' Demetrios was unmoved. 'But she already
owes some considerable sums; furs, jewellery, clothes
and so forth which I would have paid for her. After
all, it would be bad for the company image to have
the wife of Sandros Thalassis sued for debt. The sums
owing, together with what I would have paid her,
amount to slightly more than you ask for, so she'll
have a very lean year. I've given you my terms, so it's
up to you. Take them or leave them.'

'And—what makes you think I'd even consider. . . .' All Hester's carefully laid plans were crumbling into ineffectual dust and she felt on the brink of tears.

'Simple,' he broke in on her. 'You want a lot of money and you want it quickly. I shan't ask for your reasons, they don't concern me, not yet, but I can get you what you want, and it has to be on *my* terms. I'll give you half an hour to think it over, and after that you're on your own.' Again, his dark eyes gleamed with a smile and his lips curved sardonically. 'Personally, I don't give much for your chances with Vilma, not if you've a deadline. She'll stall you as long as she can and she'd cut off her right arm before she parted with one diamond or one sable coat—and as I've already explained, she won't have the cash to give you.'

'Then she can use some of her own.' Hester was sturdy. 'Her uncle left her a small fortune and she's already had one other rich husband. . . .'

Demetrios shook his head at her naïvety. 'Most of that's already spent. If one wishes to catch a prize as rich as Sandros Thalassis, one can't be mean about the quality and quantity of the bait.' There was disillusion in his eyes and a cynical twist to his mouth.

Hester covered her disappointment well, although her heart had dropped right to the soles of her high-heeled shoes. She gave a slight shrug.

'I'll need to know a bit more,' she murmured. 'It's rather a big decision to rush into and you really aren't giving me much time.' She pushed her plate aside and shook her head at his offer of a sweet. 'Just coffee, thank you. Do we talk about it now?' Nothing was going as she'd planned and hoped, and she'd been so sure. . . . Dejection settled on her, giving her mouth a sad, weary droop.

'Over coffee,' he said adamantly, and turned to give

instructions to the waiter who was hovering. 'I've ordered some little cakes and there's a wide choice of fruits and cheeses—do you want a liqueur with your coffee?'

'No, thank you.' Hester chose that moment to remember Flo's oft-repeated warnings about men who tried to get a girl drunk—it struck her as being excruciatingly funny, almost to the point of hysteria, and she choked back a desire to break into wild, uncontrolled laughter. 'But why me?'

He shrugged. 'I have to make a home here for my daughter—my present arrangements have ceased rather abruptly. Besides, I think it's about time she lived with me, and that means a female to look after her and my home.'

'But you could employ a nanny and a housekeeper,' she quibbled. 'Surely that would be better than going in for anything as binding and permanent as marriage—especially to me! You can't have a very high opinion of me.'

'My daughter needs more than a nanny and a housekeeper,' he said flatly. 'Surely you know that? She needs to be part of a family, to be loved, to be made to feel secure—no different from the other children she'll meet. You were fostered, weren't you? And you felt the difference, I'm sure.'

'No, I didn't,' she protested vigorously. 'My foster-parents were real parents to me. It wasn't until I was eighteen that I knew differently.'

'But I've no intention of fostering my daughter,' he pointed out. 'She'll live with me, in a household as regular as I can make it. As for why I've chosen you, I thought I'd made that clear—my opinion of you doesn't enter into it. You'll understand what sort of a home Kadijha needs.'

'Kadijha?' Hester raised her eyebrows. 'That doesn't sound Greek.'

'A name's a name,' he frowned. 'It's of no consequence, and I always call her Katy.'

'And that's your only reason for offering me help to get the money—and a wedding ring thrown in?' She was disbelieving, and her disbelief was justified.

'Not entirely.' Demetrios leaned back in his chair and surveyed her blandly. 'I shall expect you to give me a son.'

Hester went rigid, her face paled, but she retained her composure. 'I think this conversation would have been better conducted over a telephone,' she murmured. 'I'd have hung up on you long before now.'

'One reason I decided to have it in a public restaurant.' His mouth curved into a smile of derision. 'I knew I could rely on your behaviour in public. Are you going to accept my proposition?'

'I suppose I should be thankful you didn't say proposal,' she sniffed, 'and I suppose I should be equally grateful for your—I can't call it honesty—I think a better word would be "crudity". So it's not just for the look of things?'

'Certainly not!' This time she was sure of the derision that lit his eyes. 'Such a relationship would be unnatural—it couldn't be sustained. Either of both of us would weaken, and then there would be tearful scenes of recrimination and you'd be awash with either guilt or self-pity.'

'Neither of which would affect you, of course.' She bit into a piece of something very sweet and cloying which tasted as though it was made of nuts and honey and abandoned it after that first bite, grimacing at the sweetness.

'I certainly shouldn't feel any guilt,' he chuckled.

'Why should I, about a perfectly normal need?' He glanced at his watch. 'You've only ten minutes left to make up your mind,' he reminded her.

Very steadily Hester returned his gaze. There wasn't all that much to think about—there wasn't any other way she could think of to get a very large sum of money and to get it quickly. But she didn't want to appear too desperate; he could easily take advantage of that, reduce the pay-off or something equally disastrous.

'Make it a quarter of an hour,' she answered him lightly. 'I'll have a cup of coffee to wash away the taste of that thing,' she gestured at the plate. 'A little of it goes a long way, and when my mouth feels clean again, I'll give you an answer. Personally, I think you're asking rather a lot. You drive a hard bargain.'

'For twenty thousand pounds cash and a lifetime of security?' Demetrios shook his head and his hand reached out to cover hers where it lay on the table. The touch of his long fingers sent what felt like an electric current through her whole body and she drew a sharp breath. 'You set the fashion of time limits, I'm merely following your example, and I think the arrangement should work very well. You don't seem to find my touch distasteful.'

'You'd accept my word? Me, a self-confessed blackmailer?' Hester raised her eyebrows and watched him smile in a satisfied way.

'No,' he was bluntly rude. 'I'm a business man and I've found that promises don't pay dividends. Oh,' as he saw her angry look, 'I'll trust you with the money for a few days, but I'll make damn sure you don't doublecross me. Money is only money, but my private affairs are another matter. I'm laying myself open to your type of blackmail.'

'You're using a pretty potent type yourself,' Hester pointed out.

'Yes,' he grinned, and chuckled. 'I am, aren't I, but when I do something, I do it properly and I don't leave loose ends hanging about. My way, you get your dues but you'll have no opportunity to capitalise on your knowledge.'

'Because I've become one of your family?'

'Because I'll beat you,' he corrected. 'You shall have your retribution, but you're not the daughter of night, to pursue somebody indefinitely.'

'Daughter of night?' Hester was mystified.

'Nemesis,' he gave her a wry smile. 'She was the daughter of Hesiod—Night.'

Hester shrugged, 'Another gem to add to my Bumper Fun Book. I can see I'm going to learn a lot.'

'You accept, then?' and at her nod, 'Then you will,' he said tranquilly as though the battle was won and he had nothing left but a few mopping up operations, 'finish your coffee and we'll go.'

Hester drained her cup, getting a mouthful of bitter grounds for her pains, and at her grimace, Demetrios laughed. 'The dregs are never pleasant. Be content to sip from the top of the cup.'

'Oh, very cryptic!' and she swept past him to the door, her nose in the air and every hair of her mahogany mane bristling with outrage.

By the time he pulled the car up outside the house where she lived, her mouth was dry with fright. Suppose he demanded payment at once—her fingers crisped around her flat little bag—as proof of her good intentions? Her mind balked at even thinking about it in everyday terms. Despite her twenty-four years, nearly twenty-five—she had very little experience of men, she'd never been to bed with one before.

'I like to keep things legal and proper,' he picked up her thought, which wasn't to be wondered at—she was shaking like a leaf. 'It's the accountant in me,' he continued imperturbably. 'You'll have your money tomorrow and I shall make arrangements for our wedding. Don't try to run away, Hester, I wouldn't like our marriage to begin on a wrong note.'

With a fluid movement, he was out of the car and round to hold her door open for her. 'Goodnight,' he murmured, 'and shall we begin as we mean to go on?' There were people walking along the street, but for all the notice he took of them, they might as well have been invisible—he acted as if she and he were alone in the world. His arm was close and firm about her waist while his hand tipped up her chin and he stood for several seconds just looking down at her. 'I think we shall enjoy each other,' he drawled at last before he kissed her.

Hester had been kissed before, but this was different—as though it was a sign of total possession and she was being branded as his mouth teased her lips apart. Fighting—struggling would be no use, she knew that, and after a moment she didn't want to fight. Demetrios had drawn every bit of resistance from her until she had as much will as a doll, a thing! Deep inside her, excitement flickered and grew—a new feeling she had never experienced before. It made her want to run away so that she had to cling to him to stop herself doing it.

Then he raised his head and she heard his soft, triumphant laugh and, filled with shame, she tore herself away from him and fled up the steps to the door, where her fingers shook so much she could hardly get her key into the lock. She stood for a moment in the ill-lit hallway, feeling no satisfaction but only a cold emptiness, a need for his arms about her once more.

CHAPTER THREE

THE thing she had learned in Demetrios' arms and with his mouth on hers, stayed with Hester, occupying her mind to the exclusion of everything else until three o'clock the following day. She couldn't understand it—she was a sensible girl, practical and not given to flights of fancy, and she couldn't and wouldn't believe she'd fallen in love with a man, not Demetrios and not like that—at the drop of a hat.

Love, surely, was a thing that grew, it didn't spring full-fledged into life like this. She didn't want it anyway, it would be an inconvenience, a weak spot in her armour, and she had a shrewd suspicion she would need as much armour as she could get when she married him or she would end up a soft, malleable thing, depending on Demetrios for any little token of affection. All Flo's strictures and advice hadn't prepared her for this—it even drove Flo's dire need to the back of her mind, made it a secondary consideration.

And then, just after lunch, when she was retrieving her combs and brushes from the tiny autoclave where they had been sterilising during the lunch hour, her boss wandered into her cubicle, frowning and tut-tutting over the appointments book.

'Can you fit another lady in this afternoon, lovey? Before four o'clock?'

'I'm free from three till four, as you very well know, Crispin, so don't wave that book in front of me. You're only doing it for affect.' Hester put every other thought from her mind and smiled gently to rob the words of any hint of brusqueness. Crispin was a dear, he'd always treated her decently and she owed him a lot.

'*Not* a regular,' he grinned back at her, and tossed the pages of the book over, searching for a previous appointment without having any luck. 'But if we can convert her——' he turned back to the current page. 'Ah, here it is, a Greek lady, shampoo and blow dry—she asked for you especially.'

Hester didn't need a crystal ball. 'Mrs Vilma Thalassis,' she murmured. 'But she's not Greek, Cris, only married to one. Yes, I can take her, but frankly, I'd rather not.'

Crispin raised a fair eyebrow. 'An acquaintance, darling?'

Hester made a face. 'We haven't been introduced socially, if that's what you mean but I know her.' She was deliberately vague. Cris was a marvellous hairdresser, a coming top crimper, but he was also a gossip. It was part of his charm and most of the reason for his success.

'Good girl!' he nodded approvingly. 'I'll send her in to you and Deline can do the shampoo,' and with that, he wandered out.

'You'll probably have a complaint about me,' Hester called after his retreating back, but he pretended not to hear and she was alone again with some not very pleasant thoughts.

She wasn't relishing the appointment, it was going to be uncomfortable to say the least and provided she and her mother were completely alone—no junior popping in and out—it was bound to be an unpleasant hour. Vilma wasn't the forgive and forget type!

But at a quarter past three, when Deline handed

over the shampooed client, Hester was outwardly cool and competent. She watched her mother seat herself before the mirror and wished there were doors to the cubicles instead of curtains—then she comforted herself with the thought that Vilma would be discreet and restrained if only because there *were* curtains—she wouldn't want anybody to hear.

Vilma sat silent while Hester brushed out wet blondeness which was mainly skilfully applied highlights, but as she picked up brush and dryer, baby blue eyes met hers in the mirror and there was a venomous glow in the blue so that it looked more like chips of Polar ice.

'Demos has told me the news, and I think you've done very well for yourself.' Her mother's sneer was delicate. 'Twenty thousand of *my* money and Demos as a bonus—you're a fast worker, I'll grant you that!'

'Something I inherited from my mother.' Hester felt unsure of herself and in consequence, rather bitchy. 'But I never asked for the bonus—in fact, you're to blame for that. There wouldn't have been any if you'd paid me what I asked instead of sending round your bully boy.'

'My nephew by marriage,' Vilma corrected haughtily.

'And a great disappointment to you, I suppose,' Hester smiled serenely, and went on with her work, resisting her desire to retaliate in the only way she could—to put the blow dryer on full heat and dry out those highlights to a strawlike texture. 'Were you hoping he'd get you off scot free?'

Her mother was frank. 'I was hoping for a reduction—I can't afford to give away that much money, not out of my paltry allowance. It means I'll have to go into debt again, and Sandros can be very awkward when he's in a temper.'

Hester gazed down at her mother's beringed hands, at the heavy gold chains and bracelets she was wearing, together with what was obviously an Yves St Laurent suit—she sniffed at the fragrance of 'Joy' and crowded down her own feelings of guilt.

'You could forgo next autumn's sables,' she suggested mildly, 'or make do with last winter's wardrobe.'

Vilma ignored such a ridiculous suggestion while she allowed her brow to furrow very slightly in thought. 'I can't think why he tagged on that condition.' She raised her eyes swiftly to the mirror to catch Hester's expression. 'You aren't blackmailing him as well, are you?' There was no doubt about her mystification.

'How could I?' Hester went on brushing and blowing, determined to give nothing away. 'I've only just met him, I wasn't even aware of his existence.'

'Then all I can think of is that he made the condition to put you off.' Vilma's eyes glittered. 'You must be incredibly naïve if you think you've made a good deal. You've caused me a lot of trouble, but it's nothing to what you've laid up for yourself. Life's not going to be any bed of roses for you, so don't run away with the idea that you're home and dry without a single thing to worry about. He probably thought you'd turn him down—settle for a smaller sum—and now he'll make you pay for every penny you've extracted from me.'

'I'm shaking in my shoes.' Hester hoped her mother didn't know how true that statement was! 'What is he, some sort of old-fashioned Greek family man?'

'Much worse than that,' her mother drawled,

relishing every word. 'Hasn't he told you? He's never lived in Greece, he wasn't even born there and except for his fantastic flair for making money, I don't suppose the family would have anything to do with him at all—in the same way, they never had anything to do with his father. They both rate as outcasts, only Demos is tolerated!'

'I'll bear it.' Hester kept cool. 'Think of the advantages. He seems to control the money side of things—even you have to go to him for your allowance.' She switched off the dryer and began to brush and shape the style while the tongs heated for the side flicks. It was rather a young style for a woman of her mother's age, but on Vilma it looked good. It gave her an air of youth that matched her carefully dieted figure and her cherished complexion. Hester took a spiteful pleasure in noticing that her mother's complexion wasn't a patch on Flo's, who was at least twenty years older and had never used anything but soap and water.

'But why should he be an outcast?' she enquired gravely.

Vilma gave a little tittery laugh. 'You don't think much of me as a mother—well, the family didn't think much of *his* mother. She was Turkish!'

'That's a sin?' Hester raised her eyebrows.

Vilma displayed savage satisfaction. 'It makes him half Turkish, half devil as far as most Greeks are concerned. He hides it well, but now and then the basic cruelty shows through. He'd watch you die in agony and smile while you were doing it.'

Hester brushed it aside while a fleeting thought sped through her mind. She wondered what Demetrios had done or not done to gain Vilma's dislike. It could be because he'd cut her money, but somehow she had the impression that the bad feeling was rooted further back in time. 'I'm half you,' she said quietly, 'but I'm nothing like you, so I don't see that heredity is all that reliable a guide.'

'You'll find out,' again her mother tittered. 'I won't spoil the surprise by telling you any more. You've asked for trouble and you've got it coming! Demetrios is enough of a Greek to resent outsiders butting in and the Turk in him will see you pay for what you've done—you'll pay for every penny, in blood, I hope and don't come whining to me!'

'I don't think I'm in the habit of doing that,' Hester said gently. 'Probably something to do with never having you to come whining to—besides, the people who brought me up taught me to stand on my own feet and accept the responsibility for my own mistakes.'

'Some East End family, I believe.' Vilma was sneeringly acid. 'It shows in the way you speak. I'd advise you to have elocution lessons if you want to make a go of your new life, although, as I said, Demos isn't accepted by the family, not socially, and he doesn't bother with my circle of friends. He'll probably add you to his harem and you'll never meet anybody, so it doesn't matter a damn how you speak.'

'I'm overwhelmed by your concern for my well-being.' Hester grimaced as she brushed out the last flick and then composed her face into a cool mask as Crispin came through the curtain to stand beside her.

'Is everything satisfactory, Mrs Thalassis?' He walked all round Vilma to get the overall picture. 'Do you want hairspray?'

'I think I'd better.' Vilma's tone changed to one of bored disappointment. 'It's not as good as my usual place, I think I was misled about this girl's abilities. If I come again, I shall expect you.'

When she had gone, Crispin turned a quizzical glance on Hester. 'You didn't get on,' he murmured reproachfully. 'Instant dislikes aren't good for business, Hester.'

'A mutual antipathy,' Hester said gravely, and Crispin looked surprised.

'Now you've really shaken me, darling! I've never known that happen with you before, but if I thought you were going to make a habit of it, I suppose I should be glad you're leaving to get married, but I *do* wish you'd told me before—that you're leaving, I mean. I think I deserve better from you than a few days' notice, don't I?' He shook his head sadly. 'And then I didn't have the information from you—you left it to your feller to tell me, which he did less than half an hour ago—by telephone. It's going to put me in a spot, you've several ladies booked for next week.'

Hester felt she had enough troubles of her own without getting involved in Crispin's. 'Sorry, maestro, not my fault, truly. It's as much news to me as it is to you. Oh,' as she saw his eyebrows go up like a startled faun's, 'I knew, of course but I didn't know when, not exactly. I suppose he's arranged things more quickly than he expected.' It was the only way she could think of on the spur of the moment to explain things, and she said it with a painful smile on her face while she damned Demetrios to hell for his officious interference.

This showed how much he trusted her, not even as far as he could throw her! She gave a mental shrug; she couldn't expect much more—she'd done nothing to give him a good opinion of her, quite the reverse!

Crispin surveyed her judiciously. 'Are you thinking of working after you're married, perhaps?'

'I shouldn't think so,' Hester embroidered the truth

a bit. 'My fiancé's a widower with a young daughter, so I expect to have my work cut out for quite a while. Don't tell me I'll leave you short-staffed—you'll be able to promote another girl in my place and start a beginner. There's no shortage on the labour market.'

'I was going to promote another girl anyway.' Crispin fiddled with a tail-comb almost as if he was embarrassed. 'I'm opening another salon in Knightsbridge and I was thinking, if you had a bit of capital, I'd take you in as a partner and you could manage this place on a profit-sharing basis. You'd have been manageress here in any case, even if you couldn't put anything into the business.'

'Now you tell me!' Hester sighed disgustedly. It was what she had always wanted and the offer had come too late. 'Sorry, Cris, but I don't think my future husband would care for the idea.'

'Later on he might, so bear it in mind,' Crispin suggested. 'Leave it a while—I'll keep the offer open. These days most married women work, so wait until the old man starts finding how expensive it is to keep two on a salary which seems to buy less every week. He might change his mind!'

Hester's doorbell gave a prolonged peal and she ceased to squeeze gently at her tights which she was washing in the handbasin. With a sigh, she wiped her hands free of soapsuds and went to answer the door, knowing full well who was leaning against the bellpush.

'You'll wear out the battery,' she muttered darkly. 'There's nothing wrong with my ears.'

'Your ears——' Demetrios stepped into the hall, casually well dressed and with a folded raincoat over his arm. He put out a hand and lifted a heavy swathe of hair lying against her neck. 'I think they're charming, like the rest of you,' his finger touched her ear and she shrank away, frowning. 'Except for that bad-tempered scowl you're wearing,' he was bland.

'The sight of you makes me bad-tempered,' she scolded, while Vilma's most objectionable remark still rang in her ears—'add you to his harem'. She'd even found herself repeating it under her breath over and over again. It had one good effect, however—she wasn't in love with him any more; it had, she had decided, been a momentary infatuation, the product of relief from the nagging worry of Flo's illness and his promise to get her the money she needed. Now she was in her right mind at last.

'You say that when I've brought you your money?' His eyebrows arched and then drew together in a frown as though he sensed her withdrawal. 'I thought you'd welcome me with open arms.' He fumbled in the folds of the raincoat and produced a small brown paper carrier bag, not much larger than the sort used by chemists for prescriptions. He dangled it in front of her eyes, 'As you asked, all in cash—nothing larger than a twenty-pound note—all used and untraceable and all in a paper bag. Do you want to count it?'

'In that little thing?' Hester's face registered disbelief as she stepped past him to open the door which he had carefully closed behind him. 'I thought it would make a bigger parcel than that. However, I'll trust you, but I prefer to do the counting in private. I'm sure you wouldn't short-change me.'

It was meant to be a waspish remark, but as she said it, she knew it was true. Vilma might have done that, but not this man; he was too meticulous. From underneath her lashes she surveyed him. He was meticulous about everything—the way he dressed, the way he behaved and the way he put his propositions down on the table with no attempt to hide the bad bits.

Her fingers closed on the carrier and some but not all of her bad mood vanished. She smiled rather weakly. 'As I said, I'll trust you, and as I'm rather busy. . . .'

'. . . . I shouldn't detain you, is that right?' With his foot, Demetrios pushed the door closed again despite her efforts to hold it open. 'Shall we stop playing games with your door!' he enquired lazily. 'I'm going to win in the end and you know it.' Then with a firm hand about her upper arm, he steered her into the living room. 'Are you going to keep that amount of money in the place overnight?'

Hester hesitated; lies didn't come easily to her. She had an inventive mind, but she always stumbled over the actual telling of an untruth. 'N-no,' she hesitated slightly, 'I think I'll take it to a friend for safe keeping, that'll be the best.'

'I'll drive you wherever you want to go,' he offered helpfully. 'I don't like to think of you travelling about the city with all that money in your bag—it would be so easy for somebody to steal it.'

'My, oh, my,' she marvelled, 'aren't you the thoughtful one! So much concern for *my* money! I assure you that, if I lost it or it was stolen, I shouldn't ask for any more.'

'Which is all to the good,' Demetrios seated himself without asking, 'because you'd stand no chance of getting a replacement sum from me, and I'm sure Vilma wouldn't oblige.' He stretched his legs to a more comfortable position. 'Get your coat and we'll go.'

'What you mean is, you want to know what I'm going to do with it?'

'Quite right,' Demetrios nodded, 'and I've no intention of letting you out of my sight until I find out.'

Hester gave him a reluctant grin. 'At least you're honest. I think I'll take a chance and keep it here for the night.'

'In that case,' he countered, 'I think I should stay to see you're not robbed.' His eyes slid to the divan, made up for the daytime with a tartan throwover and a couple of cushions. 'There should be room for both of us on that,' he goaded.

'Honest and determined with it!' she snapped acidly. 'Don't you realise that it's my money now and I can do what I like with it? I don't have to tell you a thing if I don't want to.'

'You'll tell me what I want to know.' Demetrios was lazily confident.

'Oh, for crying out loud!' Her patience snapped. 'Don't you ever let go? I have my own reasons, isn't that good enough?'

'No.' He sounded mild but immovable. 'It may be your money now, but I still want to know. As your future husband, I think I should be told.'

She let loose with an expletive which would have been better deleted.

'Very crude,' he reproved, 'and coarse. I didn't know you knew such a word. Don't ever let me hear you say it again.'

Hester was defiant. She repeated it loud and clear—and then wished she hadn't. Demetrios was on his feet in one sinuous movement, his arms were round her like steel bands and she was hauled close against his broad chest. The scent of aftershave and cologne assailed her nostrils, the warmth of his body against hers made a mockery of her independence. She held his gaze defiantly for as long as she could and then, with a little moan, closed her eyes as she felt every bit of pride and independence drain away, leaving her weak and wanting.

'That's better,' he approved, releasing one arm and wiping her mouth with his handkerchief before he kissed her. It was a kind of drowning in bliss, she thought, while she was still capable of thought, that nothing she had ever heard, read or thought had prepared her for this. She shivered uncontrollably as his arms relaxed their pressure and his hands stroked and soothed, bringing her even closer to him—and then she wasn't soothed at all, she was filled with a fierce hunger, an almost unbearable need. Tears welled into her eyes at the pain of it, she gave a little sob, and suddenly he had released her and stepped back.

The movement was so swift, she almost fell, and she blinked dazedly, her eyes refusing to focus properly.

'Everything in its right place and in the correct order.' Demetrios sounded as shaken as she was, and then his voice took on the old amused tone. 'It's the accountant in me, so stop tempting, my brown-haired witch. It's going to be great and glorious, but not here and not now.'

'Oh!' The words brought her back to earth with a bump, she was no longer floating weightlessly on Cloud Nine but back in her rather third rate bedsit, the carpet worn and faded and her tights soaking in the handbasin. Looking past him, she could see into the tiny bathroom through the partially open door to where a half empty packet of soap powder balanced drunkenly on the shelf above the basin. The sight restored her to normality more quickly than if she had been suddenly immersed in cold water.

'Turning on the charm?' Her mouth felt bruised

and she lifted a shaking hand to steady her lips. 'It won't work so well next time, I'm building up an immunity.' She was tired of conflict and her shoulders sagged. 'I know a very safe place for the money—you can come with me if you like.'

She had a choice; either she could take it straight to Mia—which was what she wanted, if only to see the relief and delight which would light her foster-sister's face—or she could take it to Crispin's place, a studio apartment in Chelsea, but taking it home to Poplar would mean that Demetrios would meet Mia, and Flo wouldn't let a visitor go—especially a man who came with Hester—not without seeing him and talking to him.

Hester dismissed the Poplar idea. Flo thought her stay in Switzerland was being organised by the National Health, and although Mia knew better, knew how the money was really being obtained, she didn't know about Demetrios' conditions. Flo wouldn't stand for what she'd done and Mia would balk at this strange marriage, then all Hester's hard work would be wasted. Crispin's it should be, and at least he had a safe.

'You'll get a bit of a surprise,' she mused, thinking of Crispin's Art Nouveau décor, his Oriental cushions and mad lighting effects. 'It's my boss's place—I believe you spoke to him on the telephone today.' That reminded her of his high-handed ways. 'What right had you to tell him I was leaving—to arrange it for me?' She scowled and her eyes glittered. 'You made me look an absolute fool! You should have left it to me, and when you'd made the arrangements, I'd have given in my notice in the usual way.' She stuffed her feet into her shoes and grabbed her coat from the hook, disdaining any help with it, and finally scrabbled in her bag for one of Crispin's cards which she stuffed in his fingers with a curt, 'I'm ready. We're going to Chelsea—here's the address.'

The door of Crispin's flat was open and the strains of soul music greeted her as she stepped over the threshold, beckoning Demetrios to follow but not turning her head to see whether he did or not. Crispin, in a purple satin jumpsuit met them as he was carrying a loaded tray from the kitchenette into his living room.

'Darling!' He greeted her with obvious pleasure and then looked over her shoulder to where Demetrios stood, tall and rigid. 'Is this your man? Bring him in, do—we're having a bit of a party—no, don't run away,' as she made to turn and leave. 'It's just a few friends celebrating my new venture, all very nice types.'

'It's business.' Hester moved forward reluctantly. 'Nothing to do with your business, though. I just wondered if you'd do me a favour till tomorrow and keep this in your safe.' Her hand produced the brown paper bag which she had converted into a neat parcel.

'Mm,' Crispin thrust the tray at her, 'hold this, my sweet, have a canapé and a drink.' He gave her a droll look. 'I shouldn't do you any favours, you know—not after you've practically walked out on me, but for you, Hester, anything. Is it valuable?'

'So—so,' Hester shrugged. 'We won't keep you a minute, we don't want to intrude.'

'Who's intruding?' Crispin's fair eyebrows nearly touched his hairline. 'And why so formal? Come and meet my friends—and,' he glanced over her shoulder at Demetrios, 'wouldn't you like to introduce me? Oh, sorry, sweetie, I've left you holding the tray. Shan't be a sec—just let me get rid of it.'

The beat of soul music increased as he pushed open his living-room door—there was a babel of voices and Hester shrank from the noise. She wasn't in the mood for parties; all she wanted was to see her parcel safely tucked away and then get back to her own place.

'There!' Crispin was triumphant as he returned empty-handed, 'that didn't take long—now, let's have the introductions.'

'Crispin—Demetrios Thalassis.' She made it as brief as possible, hoping Crispin wouldn't recognise the name but knowing he would. He never forgot a client's name—he prided himself on it.

'Any relation to our new client?'

'By marriage only.' Demetrios kept it curt and Hester knew he wasn't approving of Crispin. Under her lashes she peeped at his impassive face and hastily thrust herself between them, words tripping off her tongue.

'We haven't much time, I'm afraid, so could you . . .?'

'Not joining the party?' Crispin looked disappointed and then reverted to his businesslike approach. 'Oh well, some other time, perhaps, when you're not so busy.' He led the way down the passage and opened a door into a bleak little room, strictly functional and with not a trace of Art Nouveau. 'My office and,' he felt around the parcel, 'here's the safe. What is it, money? Oh, does that mean you've changed your mind, that you're going to buy into the business after all?'

' 'Fraid not.' Hester was suitably sad as she watched him stow her precious package away and lock the small safe. 'Will you bring it tomorrow, please, I'll bank it at lunch time.'

Goodbyes were brief—Demetrios made it quite

clear that he had neither the time nor inclination to hang about. He stood in the narrow hallway, reducing its proportions to the size of a dog kennel, and he looked as if it smelled like one. His lofty superiority upset Hester so that when she seated herself in the car, she erupted in a uncontrolled fashion.

'Stuck-up pig! How dare you treat a friend of mine like that!'

'Friend?' There was a nasty note in his voice and she could hardly recognise the smiling, almost teasing man who had come to her flatlet earlier that evening.

'Yes, *friend*! Cris has been very good to me, I've worked for him since I was seventeen and he's taught me a lot. If it hadn't been for you and your machinations, I'd have been promoted manageress of the present salon when he opens the new one in Knightsbridge. . . .'

'And was that money intended to buy your way into a partnership?'

Hester choked on wrath. She and Crispin had gone alone into the office while Demetrios waited outside. 'You've been listening at keyholes to what's none of your business,' she spat. 'How low can you get?'

'Much lower, if I have to,' he answered unashamedly. 'Remember, what my wife does *is* my business!'

'But I'm not your wife yet,' she reminded him sweetly.

'Mmm,' he swerved to avoid a jaywalker and swore under his breath, 'we'll talk about that when we're back at your place—a sensible discussion's impossible in these circumstances. Is there anything to eat at your flat?'

'Baked beans on toast,' she offered icily. 'I don't go in for candlelit dinners à deux.'

'Then my place, I think.' Abruptly he changed direction at the next traffic lights and headed for Mayfair.

'Here it comes!' sighed Hester in a world-weary way. 'The big seduction scene. You men are *so* unoriginal—the same old act every time. . . .'

'Not in the least.' The change in his tone was striking and again she peeped, to find a smile of pure amusement about his mouth. 'I shall take a virgin to my marriage bed—by the way, you are one, aren't you?'

'That's for me to know and you to find out.' Hester tried to conceal her embarrassment beneath an airy layer, but her cheeks had reddened, and then, 'Oh!' as his hand found her knee and his fingers trailed upwards. 'Cut that out!' and she slapped hard at his fingers.

'Yes,' he murmured, 'I think you are,' drawling it back at her. 'You put up a sophisticated front, but underneath it you're scared to death.' She saw the white flash of his teeth as his mouth parted in a knowing smile. 'There's an automatic withdrawal, a shrinking away from the unknown, by the inexperienced.'

'Then I bet you've not shrunk from anything since you were sixteen,' she snapped waspishly. 'Would you like me to produce a medical certificate?'

'No,' he shook his head and she caught the gesture in the darkness. 'I don't like intruders on my property, even doctors. Now, be quiet until we get to the hotel.'

'*Your* property!' Hester's voice rose on a squeal of outrage. 'If I live to be ninety, I'll never be *your* propert. . . .' and she finished on a yelp of anguish as his fingers and thumb found the sensitive spots on her knee and squeezed remorselessly.

'I said be quiet!' He released her knee and she took a deep breath—his property, indeed! She'd show him! He'd have to learn she wasn't some cowed female to add to his harem and to be shut away somewhere private and labelled 'For private entertainment'! Vilma's remark still niggled at her, making her uneasy and on edge.

'You live around here,' she said when the silence between them grew too much to bear.

'In the Thalassis hotel,' he tossed the words across to her while he negotiated the traffic. 'It's a new one, only built last year, and I have the top floor, what we'd call the penthouse suite in the States.'

'Oh my, I *am* going up in the world!' She made it sound as nasty as possible. 'No wonder baked beans on toast in my bedsit was beneath you—no room service. I hope you don't expect either me or your daughter to live in a place like that. Me, I don't matter, I could live anywhere, surroundings don't mean much to me, but it's not at all the right place for a child. A child needs a home, not a hotel.'

'Then we'll find a house.' He sounded as though he was humouring her. 'Somewhere quiet, by the river, with a large garden. How would that suit?'

'Better,' she admitted grudgingly, and then, because she was cross with both him and herself, cross, worried and nearly at the end of her tether, 'What are you going to do, rub your magic lamp and summon your private genie to build one for you?'

Demetrios' hand reached out to pat her knee comfortingly. 'No, buy one. Stop being so uptight, Hester. I've told you, I shan't seduce you, we're just going to have a quiet, simple supper and a talk about the future. You can even have baked beans on toast, if you wish.'

CHAPTER FOUR

ON Monday evening, Hester climbed the steps to the Poplar flat. She climbed wearily, it had been a busy day, but physical tiredness was only part of the reason for her lagging steps. Every step she took nowadays seemed to lead her further into deception, and tonight would be the worst of all. Her mind ran back over what she intended to say, and then she decided to play it by ear. It wasn't much good rehearsing only one side of a conversation.

Flo greeted her enthusiastically. 'I thought you'd never get here, Hes! Has Mia told you the news?'

'You're off to Switzerland? It's all arranged?' Hester summoned up a look of surprise. 'Mia's managed to fix it for you?'

' 'S'right.' Flo leaned back on her pillows with a wide smile of satisfaction. 'One of the benefits of having a staff nurse in the family,' she tapped the side of her nose significantly. 'Mia knows the consultants, the nobs—talks to them in their own language.' Hester kept a straight face while she thought of her little foster-sister 'hobnobbing with the nobs'. It was a fantastic invention, one that only Flo would have believed—but meanwhile her foster-mother was continuing. 'There's ways of getting round the regulations, you know, and one of the nobs has found one. Something to do with a private health scheme—I don't know much about it 'cos I've always been on the National Health myself, but they've put me on the books of this private thing, even though I haven't paid a penny. . . .'

So that was how Mia had explained it! Hester covered a sigh of relief with a spurious yawn. It also helped to cover her wide grin of triumphant amusement. 'Sorry, Flo,' she apologised. 'It's been a busy day.'

'But you'll come and see me off tomorrow, won't you?' Flo pleaded. 'They've even arranged for Mia to come with me and stay a few days while I settle in— saves money for them, doesn't it? They don't have to send one of those expensive private nurses just for the journey.'

'There won't be any journey if you don't stop bouncing about like a two-year-old!' Hester fished in her bag for the ritual paperback and handed it over. 'Calm down and read that while I bring you a cup of tea. I'll have mine with Mia in the kitchen.'

'Clever of me, don't you think?' Mia giggled as she and Hester sat at the kitchen table. 'Isn't it a good job she's as innocent as a newborn lamb? She believed every word I told her!'

'She wants to.' Hester had a sudden flash of insight. 'I think she knows.'

'Impossible,' Mia shook her head. 'I've not said a word about you, your mother or the money, and nobody else knows.'

'I don't mean that,' Hester found it difficult to put into words. 'I mean, I think she knows it's more serious than the doctors have said. I think she knows she might die.'

Mia's thin shoulders dropped, then she straightened them and cheered up. 'You could be right, Hes, but I'm not going to think about that side of it. I've got seven days' holiday due to me and I'm taking them so

I can go with her and stay for a few days—how do I get in touch with you if I have any news?'

'Bit difficult.' Hester stirred her tea vigorously, frowning at the little mound of bubbles that broke up and swirled to the sides of the cup. 'I'm thinking of changing my bedsit.'

'Good for you! That place you're living in is claustrophobic, you're living on top of yourself—What's the new address?'

'That's the trouble, I don't know.' All Hester's carefully thought out excuses died the death. It was as she had feared, Mia wasn't asking the right questions, but she wasn't the only one to have flashes of insight; Mia had one bang on target.

'It's a man, isn't it? Go on, tell me, Hes. I'm a bit more modern and elastic than Flo. Who is he, and does he want you to move in with him?'

'He wants to marry me, but. . . .' Hester wished she could make a clean breast of it all, not get bogged down in half-truths and evasions, but she daren't. She'd have to give a name and Mia would immediately connect Thalassis—money—Thalassis; her foster-sister was no fool, nor would she accept the money under those conditions—it would pull the curtains on Flo's going to the Swiss clinic.

'And you think you've not known him long enough?' Mia asked judiciously. 'What are you going to do, have a trial run to see if you get on?'

Hester was shocked by the realisation that at least one of her ideas about Mia was way off beam—her foster-sister might be said to be bordering on the permissive, but perhaps that was better than going into a Victorian spasm!

'No-o,' she gazed at the tablecloth moodily, 'I thought I'd go away for a bit, sort things out—see if it's like the book says—"bigger than both of us". I know—ring Crispin's, but don't worry if they can't get hold of me straight away, in fact, unless it's an emergency don't bother to ring me, I'll keep in touch with you. How's that?'

'Great!' Mia smiled. 'I'm glad to hear you're human after all. I suppose it was you winning that scholarship and going off to that posh school, you never seemed the same afterwards, no games in the park, no boy-friends. . . . I know you always said it was because you had too much homework, but you never seemed as happy as you were before you went there. Be happy now, Hes.'

Hester's wedding went off without a hitch—but then, as she told herself grimly, the simpler the wedding, the less likelihood of hitches, and this, *her* wedding, was simplicity brought to a fine point. Demetrios had sent the Rolls, plus a uniformed chauffeur to bring her to the register office, he'd met her on the steps of the building, pinned a spray of tawny yellow and green orchids to the shoulder of her cream linen two-piece, exchanged her necklet of leaves for a string of pearls—putting the near gold little ornament carelessly into his pocket—and then they had gone into the marriage waiting area.

There were no guests, not even a friendly face—the witnesses were a couple brought out of the office staff, and their rather bored expressions made Hester think they'd seen it all before—too many times! She, who had been brought up in a tight community of friends and neighbours—all energetically enthusiastic and determined to make the most of any occasion, she couldn't help feeling let down. She'd been to a great many weddings—participated in the weeks of preparation beforehand, been a bridesmaid and whooped it up at receptions and the 'knees-ups' afterwards. Compared with even the poorest she'd known, this, her own, was incredibly drab—it didn't mean anything to her and she didn't feel married. When she and Demetrios emerged into the street once more, there was only the wide, heavy gold band on her finger to assure her it had all been real.

'Smile!' Demetrios made it a warning whisper out of the corner of his mouth as they came down the steps after the pitiful ceremony, and she raised her eyebrows at the sight of a couple of photographers.

'You arranged this?' she said without moving her lips which were stretched into a painful smile.

'No.' The flashes went off and she blinked involuntarily. His hand was under her elbow and he steered her competently to the waiting car. 'Somebody must have been in during the week and read the notices—the gossip column writers keep an eye on things like that—looking for something worth printing. Those two have a scoop, although they won't be sure until the pictures have been processed and gone through the hands of the writers.'

With a brusque nod, he dismissed the waiting chauffeur, who wandered off into oblivion, like a bit part player leaving the stage, and held the car door open for her.

'Ugh!' Hester gave a little shiver of distaste and then comforted herself with the thought that neither Flo nor Mia would see tomorrow's papers. 'But newspaper photographs are always bad—I shan't be recognised, thank heavens!'

'You seem ashamed of what you're doing.' Demetrios sounded more amused than offended.

'I'm certainly not dancing for joy,' she snarled softly,

'and that reminds me——' She put her fingers to her throat where the pearls rested. They felt smooth and silky but incredibly heavy and cold. 'May I have my necklet back, please?'

'It means that much to you?' and at her nod, he drove in complete silence until he reached the house where she had her bedsit and then stopped the car without making any move to get out. He simply turned and looked at her.

Hester felt threatened and her eyes hunted for the button that controlled the central locking system, but it was out of her reach. She watched, almost hypnotised, as he reached into his pocket to bring out the necklet and she saw his hand clench over it and contract into a fist. When he opened it, the fragile leaves lay crushed in his palm. Without a word, he dropped the mangled remains in her lap.

'Put it away—or better still, throw it away, I don't ever want to see it again!'

Hester fought back tears. Flo and Mia had given it to her last Christmas. As far as value—actual monetary worth was concerned, it didn't rate highly, but she treasured it. Flo was an avid 'catalogue' buyer and Mia had described the hours Flo had spent searching through the highly coloured pages for something pretty that didn't cost too much. Now it was ruined, and she thought she'd never forgive Demetrios for that.

Sorrow gave way to anger and her hands went to the back of her neck, her fingers busy with the small diamond-set gold fastener. It wouldn't open and she tugged viciously until she felt something give, the silk thread snapped and pearls went bouncing and rolling over the floor of the car.

Still in complete silence, she dragged the broken

threads, still holding the intact clasp together, from about her neck and dropped them on his knee. When she judged her voice wouldn't tremble, her tightly folded lips parted.

'Vandal!' She spat the word at him. 'I know that as far as you're concerned my little leaves were rubbish, but I'm not like you, I don't value things for what they cost—and this,' she displayed the ruined leaves, touching them with gentle, trembling fingers, 'this was irreplaceable. It was given me in love and I'd have valued it if it had been bought from Woolies. You'll never be able to give me anything one quarter as valuable or precious.' Her voice broke. 'P-pick up your pearls if you w-want them. G-grovel for them! I'll never wear them again. Now open this car and let me out!'

'Where do you think you're going? You're now my wife, remember?'

'So I am,' she sounded bleak, 'but that doesn't mean we've been stuck together with glue. For your information, I'm going to hell, come with me if you want and I hope you enjoy the trip.'

She lurched against the door and it flew open, nearly sending her headlong on to the pavement, but she recovered quickly, dashing into the house and up the stairs as though the devil was at her heels—which he was; she could hear him just behind her and when she halted at her door to burrow in her bag for the key, he was beside her. No horns, forked tail or even a suspicion of a cloven hoof, of course—such outward signs weren't necessary. To anybody else, he was just a tall, well built, good-looking man, well dressed and in complete control of himself—but she—she'd just had a glimpse of what lay beneath the surface, and it frightened her!

She envied him that control. Hers had slipped and

she was vaguely ashamed of her behaviour; it didn't go with the image she wanted to project—that of a self-possessed young woman with a skin as thick as a rhinoceros's, somebody who couldn't be hurt. With an enormous effort, she grabbed at her self-control so that when he held out his hand for the key, she could drop it into his palm with studied nonchalance and stand quietly while he opened the door for her. Her cases stood ready packed in the hallway and there was a medium sized cardboard carton in the middle of the living-room floor. Silently Demetrios picked up the cases and took them down to the car, coming back to look at the carton with disfavour.

While he was gone, Hester had been tempted to lock the door against him and stay there, but reason prevailed. Without those cases, she would have nothing to wear and nowhere to go except back to Poplar—which was unthinkable. She didn't want anything she'd done to even touch the edges of Flo's life. Look on this as a change of employment, she reasoned with herself. A different environment, different conditions and different duties—it would be easier that way.

'You don't want this stuff.' Contemptuously he kicked at the carton, which toppled over and disgorged her four cushions, covered with Mia's crocheted wool, and a couple of stuffed toys—a koala bear and a black lamb that Flo had made for her from offcuts of beaver and Persian lamb.

'Where I go,' she said sullenly, 'they go. I won't move a step without them!'

He picked up the two toys and examined them, smoothing down the koala's well worn fur and running a gentle finger over the lamb which was not so well worn. 'Have it your way.' All signs of temper were gone and he sounded quite amiable. 'Come on, madam wife, I don't know about you, but I'm starving!'

In the underground carpark of the hotel, Demetrios frowned as he put a small key into the lock of the private lift which stopped only at the kitchens before it went on to the top of the building. The key wouldn't turn because the small illuminated arrow over the door showed in the 'up' position. To Hester this meant nothing, but seemingly, he was displeased.

'Arrogance!' she chided him bitterly. 'Not everything's set for your convenience.'

Evidently she'd upset him again, because he looked at her out of an expressionless face with hard, angry eyes.

'My convenience has nothing to do with it,' he said between his teeth. 'And if you haven't worked out what it means. . . .' He shrugged, pressed the 'call' button and she heard the whine of the lift on the way down. When it stopped, he ushered her inside, the door closed and in the confined space she heard his voice like the trumpet of doom.

'Where were you yesterday? I called three times, but each time you were out. Finally your landlady told me you'd left very early in the morning, saying you wouldn't be back until late.'

'Out!' She was brief but dignified.

'I also tried to contact your ex-employer,' his voice became silky. '*He* seemed to have disappeared as well. All I received in the way of information was that he couldn't be reached.'

'So,' Hester shrugged as the lift stopped and she walked out into the corridor, 'you add two and two together—in this case, one and one. It doesn't matter if you get the wrong total because the answer's bound to be right if *you've* done the addition.' She was lofty in her displeasure.

She could have explained—that she'd been at the airport, seeing Flo and Mia off to Switzerland—that she had come back to Town, done a bit of shopping, lunched in the cafeteria of a department store and then gone on to Poplar where she had called at the housing offices, paid Flo's rent for three months ahead and then spent the rest of the day cleaning and polishing the flat. That her only company had been a garrulous neighbour from across the hall who had come offering to do the small amount of washing and water the pot plants.

As for Crispin, she knew very well where he would have been—knee-deep in decorators and suppliers of salon fitments, going from one wholesaler to another until he found just what he wanted at the price he was willing to pay. He'd have spared no effort and time would have meant nothing to him. But Hester wasn't going to give her new husband this information.

'As of eleven o'clock this morning,' she said icily, 'you have the right to know where I am, what I'm doing and how many times I blow my nose. But yesterday, that doesn't come within your orbit. Yesterday, I was free and over twenty-one and what I did was my own affair. It had nothing to do with you!' And without waiting for a reply, she stalked in the direction of the door to his suite, where she paused with her hand on the doorknob. Now she knew what Demetrios had meant when he'd been so curt about the position of the lift; it had been used by somebody coming up to his apartment and not sent down again. There was a murmur of voices from within and her nostrils caught the elusive but potent fragrance of 'Joy' with underneath it a heavier, more exotic perfume.

'We have visitors.' She turned to look at him where he was following her. 'Is this where the act begins, or do we continue to scratch each other's eyes out in public?' She paused, still with her hand on the door. 'Let's see what we know about them,' she sniffed again. 'My dear little mother—do you think she's called to wish me happiness? And there's another woman with her. Slightly younger, I think, and rather an exotic type.'

'Second sight?' Demetrios put a hand on her arm and she brushed it away.

'No, but I've got a nose like a bloodhound.' Her bad temper never lasted long and now she was grinning widely at her own thoughts. 'It's an advantage in any part of the beauty trade, having a nose like mine. Ladies rarely look the same when they're undergoing treatment, yet they expect to be recognised immediately. I always use my nose, it's infallible.'

'And what if several ladies use the same perfume? Demetrios moved closer, seeming interested.

Hester snorted at such ignorance. 'No perfume smells the same on different women, it's to do with the acids on the skin. Well,' she demanded, 'what's it to be, war or sweetness and light? Do we fight or do I play the subservient little wife? I'm afraid I can't blush to order and I'm oversized for looking demure. . . .'

'Just control that too ready tongue,' Demetrios pulled her close, his arm about her waist, 'and you could try looking adoring.'

'Miracles *do* take a little longer,' she quoted as he pushed the door open.

Hester hadn't liked the apartment much when she'd visited it before. It was, like most hotel accommodation, impersonal, a triumph of decorating and furnishing but belonging to nobody. Cushions, creaseless and immaculate, were set on the chairs and couches, looking as though they'd never been leant on, and each flower arrangement was a set piece without one bloom out of place, and even Vilma and her companion hadn't disturbed the awful regularity of everything.

Vilma was sitting on one of the couches, her chic little suit just matching her baby blue eyes, and the woman beside her—Hester immediately identified as the leading character in this ridiculous stage set, putting her in the 'other woman' role. Her eyes sparkled as she decided that Demetrios' past had caught up with him—and yet, her glance flicked to his face, taking in not only his lack of expression but also the whole aura of him—he was as much surprised as she. It *was* the past catching up, but, past or present, it had nothing to do with her, and she kept her smile going while the 'other woman' sprang lightly to her feet and ran gracefully across the room to fling herself on Demetrios' chest.

Hester moved aside, detaching herself from his arm while she murmured, 'You need both hands for this,' in a hardly audible whisper. She was rewarded by a tight, almost apologetic smile which illuminated his dark face for the space of a heartbeat before he looked down at the crown of the woman's black, glossy hair.

'Athene,' he said softly and on a note of surprise. 'What are you doing in London?'

Athene didn't answer, not immediately. Instead she wound slender arms about his neck—Hester caught a glimpse of small white hands with long fingernails painted a deep coral pink twisting in his hair, clutching at it almost feverishly—then his head was pulled down and the woman raised herself on tiptoe to fasten her deep coral pink mouth on his.

Hester darted another glance at her mother and saw the smile of satisfaction that stretched Vilma's mouth while her baby blue eyes glittered with triumph and the message came over loud and clear. This was a put-up job! Somehow Vilma had known about the wedding—she had summoned Athene and then come here, too late to stop the marriage but not too late to throw a damned great spanner in the works.

Athene moved back from Demetrios, still clinging to his shoulders. Her eyes were huge, dark and slumbrous and there was a faint flush on her ivory cheeks as she continued to gaze at him as if he was the only man in the world—as though she was eating him. Hester moved, but only to open her bag and produce a man-sized tissue which she stuffed into her husband's fingers.

'You need this,' she told him sotto voce while she gazed pointedly at his mouth, now smeared with coral pink lipstick. 'I don't think the colour suits you.' Just for a moment she thought she detected a smile of pure amusement in his eyes and then decided she'd imagined it as he wiped his mouth. 'There's some on your collar as well,' she reproved in a wifely fashion. 'You'll need to change that shirt.'

This time she was sure of the amusement but not so sure of its purity. There was a mocking quality to it and in his voice as well.

'It can wait for a few minutes, darling. I'd like you to meet Athene, she's by way of being a distant cousin.' Sardonic eyes glinted at her. 'Vilma, of course, you already know.' He assumed the air of a man vastly pleased with himself. 'Athene, this is my wife, Hester. We were married less than a hour ago, so you can be the first to congratulate us,' and then, what Hester decided was his basic cruelty showed through. 'I'm afraid you've arrived at an inopportune moment—we'd hoped to have the rest of the day to ourselves.'

Hester gave Vilma credit for a great deal of savoir-faire. Her mother's small figure stiffened and her hands curled into claws, but the muscles of her face remained relaxed. She had engineered this scene to hurt her daughter, but her daughter showed no signs of being hurt—well, there was always another time. Vilma's mouth, lipsticked to a delicate pink, still held on to a small smile, although she drooped her eyelids to hide the gleam of chagrin in her eyes. But the effect of his words on Athene was much more dramatic.

'Married!' she gasped with something like pain. 'But I told you, Demos—we always said we'd wait—I thought you'd wait for me—it was an arrangement between us. Oh, Demos,' the soft voice almost groaned his name, 'you're cruel!'

Athene's English wasn't all that good and Hester wondered why she used it, but when the woman turned to her, she understood. The dark eyes were no longer slumbrous, they were hard and dead, like pieces of polished jet. Hester had been meant to understand every word!

'Forgive me,' Athene almost cooed the words and then went into an explanation which did nothing to mend matters. 'A long time ago, when we were very young—Demos and I—but of course, we've grown up now and things have changed—Demos has changed,' she implied that she hadn't, 'but I'm very pleased he has married at last, and I hope you'll both try to be happy.'

'Thanks,' Hester said dryly, it was all the hope was worth, and she turned to her husband. 'I'm sure we could all do with a drink and some coffee. There's no hurry for lunch, is there?'

'You want a drink, Hester?' His eyebrows rose.

'Yes, please,' she answered sedately. 'Brandy, I think. It's been a very traumatic morning and I need something to steady my nerves.'

'Champagne would be more appropriate,' he murmured as he passed her on the way to the phone.

'Then I'll have both,' she muttered back defiantly, 'I feel like getting sloshed.'

Hester sank into a chair and sipped at the two teaspoonsful of brandy which Demetrios had allowed her while they waited for the coffee and champagne to be sent up from the kitchens. Nobody seemed to expect her to take any part in the conversation or make an effort to entertain the unexpected guests, and neither Vilma nor Athene showed any desire to communicate with her—Vilma had little to say and Athene concentrated on Demetrios to the exclusion of all else—chattering to him softly in Greek. From the reminiscent tone of her voice Hester deduced they were reliving their youth.

Oddly, this behaviour didn't upset her, it soothed—she was glad of a temporary cessation of hostilities, and if it hadn't been for Vilma's inimical gaze, she would have been at peace with the world, but as the waiter arrived with a trolley of coffee and two champagne bottles nestling in ice buckets, she came back to life and summoned a smile from thin air.

Nobody was going to know she felt out of her depth, that all this—the businesslike marriage, the mockery of a celebration drink—was upsetting her, that she longed to run screaming from the room. Instead, she drained the last few drops of brandy in her glass, accepted a glass of champagne and put on a bright, rather forced gaiety.

'I know,' she enthused, 'let's all have lunch together. A sort of celebration—I don't think I feel really married yet. Could the kitchens run to that, do you think, Demetrios? I don't expect a wedding cake, but I'd like a few of the usual trimmings.' She paused, knowing her speech was jerky and forced but grimly determined to continue. 'You don't have to run away, do you?' and she fixed Vilma with an icy stare, daring her to say 'Yes'.

Demetrios shrugged and again went to the phone to order so that she didn't know whether he was pleased or not, and she called herself a coward to be so obvious about not wishing to be left alone with him. Hester didn't want that, not yet—the longer it could be delayed the better she would be pleased. Being alone with him had assumed the proportions of a nightmare—the equivalent of torture, and the thought of it made her shiver despite the more than adequate central heating and air-conditioning.

After a lunch of smoked salmon and salad which was rounded off with a hastily contrived gâteau decorated with discreet little silver bells and horse-shoes—and during which Hester had drunk three large glassfuls of a dry white wine and endured a toast that mopped up the last of the remaining champagne—Demetrios dropped beside her on a couch, murmuring words in her ear, words which were inaudible to the others.

'You've nothing to fear but the thought of fear,' and she wondered how she could be that transparent; she hoped nobody else had noticed.

'Thanks,' she spoke quickly and softly, without moving her lips, 'that's all I need! I thought I was doing a good job of hiding my feelings,' and then, 'I'm not used to being in such exalted company.' The champagne bubbles were still fizzling in her blood, giving her a false courage. 'I'll try to hide it.'

'Then don't shrink when I touch you.' The words came close to her ear, his breath stirring the short hairs on the back of her neck and he slid an arm about her to pull her closer—as close as her rigid body would allow. 'Give,' he ordered. 'Don't be so stiff.'

'I can't,' she mouthed back at him desperately. 'I think I'm going to have hysterics!'

'Not yet,' he warned, 'save them for later when we're alone,' and then their little private conversation was interrupted by Vilma, being determinedly gay.

'No tête-à-têtes, please—not now, you can leave that till later. I've just had an idea—I'll give a party for you tonight. It won't be a glittering affair, just a few friends who are available at such short notice.' She paused fractionally as a swift glance passed between her and Athene and the younger woman gave a barely perceptible nod. Hester noticed the exchange, the drinks seemed to have heightened her awareness—she wondered if it had escaped Demetrios, and she was going to give him an enquiring look when Vilma continued:

'Sandros would never forgive me if I didn't do something to mark the occasion.'

'So kind of you, my dear aunt.' Demetrios' voice was like dark, liquid honey—it smoothed out the rough patches. 'But it's impossible, I'm afraid. By all means give a party if that's what will please my uncle, but Hester and I have other arrangements.' His hand found hers and he gently rubbed the new wedding ring with the ball of his thumb. 'We're leaving in a couple of hours.'

Not only did the honey soothe, it also served to gloss over his implacability—making it almost acceptable.

Hester had never had much time for what she called 'macho' men, but she had to admit they had their advantages. Vilma didn't argue, but she and Athene both dallied so that it was nearly half an hour later before they left and Hester was approaching screaming point. But she maintained her smile through it all, and when her husband came back from seeing their visitors into the lift, he surprised her with a compliment.

'You did very well through a trying time.'

Her eyebrows, slim and arched, shot up. 'You found it trying as well? That's a comfort! I thought I was on my own, but think nothing of it,' she shrugged. 'I just thought beautiful thoughts. . . .'

'While you pined for your lost freedom? Or were you pining for that man called Crispin?'

'Back to square one,' she snapped. 'How many times do I have to tell you, Cris is my friend. He's not interested in anything but his career. He's determined to get to the top, that's all that matters to him.' She shrugged. 'I don't suppose I'll ever see him again.'

'No,' Demetrios smiled as he pulled her towards him, 'I don't think you will. Remember what I said about intruders on my property.'

'And that's another thing,' Hester struggled against him ineffectually, 'I can't think of myself as *your* property, so I'd be obliged if you—if you. . . .' The rest of it was lost as his mouth came down on hers, at first featherlight, and then the pressure increased while his hand undid the buttons of her fitted jacket and found the softness of her breast. The touch of his fingers set every nerve in her body screaming and she jerked back in his arm as though she'd been stung. 'No!' It came out explosively, part fear and part an unnameable excitement. 'No,' she repeated with less force—less certainty.

'Of course not.' Demetrios was holding her much more loosely, she could have escaped had she really wanted to, but she felt too exhausted to do anything. 'Once more,' he smiled at her wryly, 'this is hardly the time or the place. Shall we look at your cases? You need one packed with sufficient to last you for a week, ten days at the most.'

The abrupt change in his manner confused her and she felt slightly disappointed that he should be so calm when she was a quivering mass of nerves.

'Tropical or arctic?' she enquired with as much aplomb as she could summon at a moment's notice. 'I mean, do I take bikinis or fur boots?' and then, 'We *are* going away? You didn't just say that to get out of Vilma's party?'

His laugh surprised her. 'Whenever possible, I tell the truth, it saves a lot of bother,' and at her understanding nod, 'We're flying out to Athens tomorrow morning, a very early flight, so tonight we're staying at a hotel close to the airport, but not too close, we don't want to be kept awake all night by planes overhead.'

Hester looked at him gravely. 'If that's the only thing liable to keep me awake,' she returned, 'I shan't worry!' She said it stoutly and with considerable emphasis. 'Before we go,' she added, 'I think I'll dispense with the floral tribute.' She unpinned the orchids and stuffed them into one of the set pieces which decorated the room. 'I hope our marriage lasts longer and looks happier than the flowers you gave me. They're wilting already.'

CHAPTER FIVE

HESTER stirred and turned over to see a black head on the pillow beside her. Demetrios' eyes were open and watching her every move, almost searching her face as though he would know what she was thinking.

'Was it good?' he asked lazily.

The question brought back memories that made the blood beat more quickly in her veins and the colour sweep up to mantle her face. She recalled his expert lovemaking, the thing he had stirred within her—a thing which had grown with every caress until it clawed at her insides, demanding satisfaction. She had hoped to be able to control it, this wild hunger but it had been uncontrollable so that now, there wasn't a part of her he didn't know, hadn't touched, kissed and fondled.

She turned her head to the window—but that had been last night, a hot passion in the night, an appetite to be fed, a need to be satisfied; but now it was morning, with the sky a faint, clear blue and a weak sun climbing the sky with no warmth in it. Hester shivered and drew the covers more closely about her naked body.

'I don't know,' she said as though she was really thinking about it and not just saying the first hurtful thing which came into her mind. 'How *could* I know? Unlike you, I don't have any standard of comparison.'

'Which is just as it should be.' Demetrios wasn't a whit abashed and he turned on to his back, pushing back the covers and putting his hands behind his head. The movement disclosed his wide chest and the dark curling hair that covered it—hair which had tickled her nose last night—it was silly how she could remember a little thing like that. She stole a glance at his profile outlined against the white of the pillow—one dark eye, almost hidden beneath a drooping lid with the thick fringe of lashes for a curtain, his nose, rather big and with a flaring nostril, the sensual curve of his mouth and his uncompromising chin, now a faint blue in the morning light.

If she touched it now, it would rasp beneath her fingers, but last night it had been as smooth as silk. Her brows furrowed as she pondered whether there could possibly be some sort of sex maniac lurking beneath her calm, practical exterior—she, Hester Marsh, who'd never been very much interested in men! Her thoughts went wandering on, over her memories of the rest of his body—the flat stomach, the narrow hips, long powerful legs—the thing stirred inside her and she bit her lip in desperation as he curled an arm about her.

'I tried to make it good for you—to be as gentle as I could. I know it isn't always satisfactory the first time for a woman. . . .'

'My misfortune—being one, I mean.' She kept it light as though he hadn't carried her up to heaven and leapt with her into a whirling abyss of the sweetest pain she had ever known—so sweet, it had ceased to be a pain and become bliss. Physical gratification was one thing, she argued it out with herself, but surely there was more to love than that, there *had* to be, and so far, she had known nothing of that softer, sweeter side. Maybe for Demetrios, it didn't exist. She could have wept at the thought, and to cover her emotion, she became practical and consoling.

'Never mind, I daresay you did your best!' She glanced at her watch, rather surprised to find it still going; surely everything should have stopped dead in its tracks last night. 'It's half past six and you said the plane took off at nine. Don't we have to be there a while beforehand? Perhaps we'd better start getting ready.'

'Oh, God,' he rolled over onto his face and from the pillow, his voice came muffled, 'I've married a practical woman!'

'Certainly,' she kept her voice flat and precise. 'That was the object of the exercise, wasn't it? I could hardly do the job you've lined up for me if I was an empty-headed little flibbertigibbet. By the way,' she nodded at the dressing table, 'there are those pearls, I picked them up, although I shouldn't have, not after the way you treated my necklace. I've tied them up in a hankie, you'd better put them somewhere safe,' and she turned her back so she wouldn't see him slip out of bed. The sight of so much completely nude flesh might upset her libido and bring on a strong attack of the lusts!

The brown boat, tied up now to a bright orange buoy and floating serenely on the wine-dark sea, had come to rest at last and Hester pulled herself up the narrow, steep little companionway that led from the small cabin, to emerge on the deck with a sigh of relief.

She hadn't really trusted this small craft, and although Demetrios had assured her there was a diesel engine for emergencies, it seemed he preferred the sail. As soon as they were clear of the harbour at Piraeus, he had cut the engine and hoisted the rust-red, almost triangular sail.

'Mediterranean rig,' he had caught her doubtful,

apprehensive look at the bellying canvas, 'a descendant of the old lateen sail and quite safe in these waters. One man can handle it easily,' he assured her.

'Hmm, I thought you could have run to a proper yacht,' Hester answered acidly. 'When I climb out of this cockleshell, I'm going to smell of fish!'

'Sardines, a few herring and the occasional octopus,' he corrected. 'Who did you think you'd married, one of the Onassis clan?'

He had changed out of his conservative travelling clothes into a pair of jeans and a tee-shirt—and he wore nothing beneath them! He'd done it in the small cabin, in front of her—in front of her back which she had turned on him with a makebelieve insouciance—unashamed of nudity. 'Change yourself,' he'd advised, 'then you won't mess up that dress. It suits you, I like it.'

'When I can have a bit of privacy, I will.' Her nose had wrinkled fastidiously. 'I'm not used to all this togetherness,' but he had only laughed at her modesty, his hands on her shoulders, turning her away from the small porthole out of which she had been looking— turning her back to face him. He had shifted his grip so that he had a hand free and begun to undo the buttons of her yellow cotton shirtwaister, and his eyes had gleamed with appreciation as he had pushed the dress from her shoulders. He had hooked a long finger into her front-fastening bra and tugged gently while watching the warm tide of embarrassment stain her cheeks.

'Get it off,' he'd advised. 'It's going to be hot and you're not used to it. You'll perspire and all this confining stuff will bring you out in a rash.'

The little hook which secured the garment parted and she had struggled to pull the two halves together, but he had only laughed again. 'Nice,' he'd teased, his hand cupping the soft weight of her breast. 'Quality *and* quantity—I'm a fortunate man!' And with an abrupt movement, he had gone and she was alone, her tongue cleaving to the roof of her dry mouth and her breast throbbing from his touch.

Angry with him—but mostly with herself for being so easily roused, she'd scrabbled through her case for a tee-shirt and a pair of shorts, meanwhile casting doubtful glances at the bra. Demetrios was right, it was hot and going to be hotter, there seemed to be little air in the tiny cabin and already her body was covered with a film of perspiration. As she changed, she measured up the two bunks with her eye—too narrow, she decided, and felt a vicarious satisfaction—and anyway, she'd have the place to herself. Somebody had to drive the boat or whatever one did with boats—which reminded her, she didn't even know where she was going.

'An island,' he had answered when she had made her way on deck to phrase the question politely, formally and in a chilly little voice. 'Very small, too small to have a name. It's one of the Naxos group and we'll be there in about fourteen hours. There's food in the galley, enough for an evening meal, and some fruit and bread for breakfast. There's some wine as well, although you can make some coffee if you want it, there's a small spirit stove in the galley. Better let me do that,' he advised. 'The stove's a bit temperamental and I don't want you burning us down to the water line.'

After an evening meal of cold meat and fruit, eaten alfresco under the shadow of the sail, and after the sail had been stowed and the engine nudged into life, Hester had gone down to the little cabin and looked longingly at the narrow bunks. They looked very comfortable and the pillows, when she had punched one of them experimentally, were soft but heat and the lack of air drove her back on deck, the pillow in her hand and a blanket trailing behind her. Darkness had fallen much more quickly than it did in England, and she dragged the blanket about her and made herself comfortable on the planking.

'You won't lose your way?' After she'd said it she could have kicked herself for sounding so ingenuous, but Demetrios, seeing her bewildered gaze on the empty seas around them, nodded understandingly.

'No, sweetheart, I shan't lose my way.' He had looked down at her as she had hooked the pillow into a more comfortable position. 'I'd join you, but one of us has to see we go in the right direction or we'll end up in Africa.'

Some time during the night, she had woken and had felt terror rising in her; she would have given all she had for the sight of a London bus and the feel of a pavement under her feet, but there had been the comforting glow of Demetrios' cigarette in the darkness and she'd gone back to sleep, feeling perfectly safe despite her unaccustomed surroundings.

Now she was scrambling out of the little dinghy which had bobbed along behind them all of the way, secured by a light line from the stern, and she struggled her way up some steps, roughly cut and slippery, to a solid rock platform hewn out of the same rock. An old man and two donkeys were waiting there, the donkeys wearing straw hats through which their large, furry ears poked, waggling now and then to set the tassels which ornamented their cone-shaped coverings swinging.

'One of them's for you.' Demetrios had finished greeting the old man and was busy loading the cases on to the larger donkey. He pointed at the smaller of the two animals. 'That one.'

Hester approached it cautiously, walking round to what she called the front end where, under the brim of the ridiculous straw hat, two large, beautiful, wise and long-suffering eyes looked at her sadly.

'*You're* going to carry me?' she murmured, and the donkey drooped its head in patient resignation. She walked round to the back of the animal and slapped gently at a thickly coated flank—a cloud of dust rose and hung in the warm, still air and she glanced down at her long legs, very chic in narrow tan cotton pants. 'Not until you've been Hoovered, you won't,' she muttered, and turning to Demetrios, 'It's not *big* enough—and anyway, I'd rather walk. It'll be good for me, stop me getting fat!' And then she blushed as his eyes slid over her, lingering on the curves of her breast and hips.

'You've got something there,' he agreed amiably. 'An hour-glass figure—it would be a pity if the sand all ran to the bottom. It's a long way, mostly uphill, and the track's rough, but Aphrodite will think she's in heaven with nothing to carry. I'll put your case on her back so she remembers she has to work for a living.'

The old man approached her and offered a plastic bottle of liquid and she thanked him. '*Parakalo,*' she said hesitantly, and was rewarded with a smile which deepened the sun browned wrinkles.

'You speak Greek?' Demetrios sounded surprised.

'Only please and thank you,' she shook her head, 'and I can't always remember which is which. I came on a package tour about three years ago. The usual thing—Athens, the Acropolis and about four trips to places of interest, but at least I saw the Acropolis, I even walked around it—I wasn't hustled out of a plane, into a taxi and whisked through to Piraeus at the speed of light,' she added in an injured tone. 'I even went out on my own one day and tried to have a meal in a café in Omonia Square, but all the places were full of men, there wasn't a table anywhere without men stuffing themselves, and it was only half past eleven in the morning!'

Demetrios' lips twitched, but he merely pointed at the bottle and advised her to save the contents for later. 'Since you won't ride, you'll probably need it.'

The sun was hot on her back and already she could feel trickles of perspiration running in the hollow between her breasts—the track was more than rocky, it was dangerous; loose stones slipped under her rope-soled sandals and she twisted her ankle several times and cast an envious look at little Aphrodite—a ridiculous name for a donkey—whose neat little hooves clicked along surefootedly beside her. Within half an hour, she was exhausted and called a halt.

'I'm going to have a rest and a drink,' she stated firmly as she grabbed at the plastic bottle, retiring with it to the side of the track where she rested herself with her back against half a mountain. 'This isn't my idea of a Greek island, it's more like part of some weird lunar landscape! I've heard that Greeks, when they've made enough money, always try to buy themselves an island. Did you buy this one? Because if you did, you've been had!'

The fresh, slightly warm lemon juice ran down her throat like milk and Demetrios took the bottle from her, wiping the mouth before he drank. She watched the movement of his throat as he swallowed—a throat that seemed browner already, whereas she—she glanced down at her bare arms—she was going an unbecoming red.

Another half hour's walking and the track took a sharp twist and descended slightly to a huge, bowl-like depression where great rocks reared dark and menacing against the deep blue of the sky and in the middle of them, a gold-coloured pinnacle like a flat-topped cone thrust upwards.

It was an awesome sight and Hester gazed at it fearfully. 'Oh, very picturesque,' she said chattily. 'I think I've seen something like this before. I can't remember the name of the place, I think the guide called it Meteora, and there was a monastery on top of the highest rock.'

'There's one on top of this one,' Demetrios waved to where she could just make out the glint of a red-tiled roof that crowned the peak. 'We live up there.'

'In that other one,' she muttered darkly, 'they had a basket thing on ropes to pull people up.'

'So do we,' he grinned at her, 'but there are also some steps, six hundred to be precise.'

'And you keep your poor little daughter up there? How mad can you get?'

'Poor little, safe little daughter,' he corrected. 'Two years ago, when we lived near Catanzaro, in Calabria, there was a kidnap attempt. Here, she's safe from things like that.'

'Sorry,' Hester wiped perpiration from her forehead. 'You *did* say six hundred steps?'—unbelievingly—'I'll be dead before I get to the top!'

'You only need to climb the last hundred,' he comforted her. 'There's an easier way, it's well hidden and it takes a little longer, but,' he urged her to where

Aphrodite was head down among the sparse vegetation, 'you'll have to ride, so get into the saddle.'

It was just like riding the donkeys on the sands at Margate, only now she wasn't a child any more, she was a full grown woman and her feet dangled to within six inches of the ground on either side. 'The latest safety model,' she quipped to cover her embarrassment, and then, 'The things we'll do for money! Come on, my fiery steed, let's see what you're made of!' and Aphrodite moved off quickly towards what looked like a crack in the rocks.

'I honestly never thought I'd do it.' Hester pushed her way through a wooden gate set in a stone arch to enter a small courtyard. 'You did say only a hundred, didn't you? I could have sworn it was nearly a thousand!' She staggered theatrically across to a stone seat set conveniently near and flopped down on it to remove her sandals with a groan of relief and lift her face to the cool breeze. 'If I lived here, I'd never go down,' she said succinctly. 'I couldn't face climbing back up again!'

'You're out of condition.' Demetrios stood over her and she noticed he wasn't even breathing heavily, but anything else he would have said was cancelled out by the squeak of a door and a glad cry. Hester lifted her eyes to see a wooden door, bleached to a pale grey by sun and wind, being flung open and a child running across the courtyard. She blinked, gasped and felt her heart drop right down to the soles of her feet.

Athene! It was her first thought. Of course, it wasn't Athene, the size and shape were wrong, but in everything else, here was Demetrios' 'distant cousin' running to greet them. The hair, the shape of the face, eyes, mouth, even the lift of the chin and the grace of the flying figure, they all shrieked 'Athene'. Suddenly there

was no warmth in the sun and the breeze, which had
been cool and refreshing, became an icy blast to send
goosepimples down her back and make her shiver.

Her thoughts were muddled as she tried to work out
the implications—so muddled that nothing made
sense. Athene had said she expected Demetrios to wait
for her—instead he had married her, Hester, rushed at
it like a bull at a gate. If he'd waited only a week, until
Athene had arrived in London, would it have made
any difference? She gave up, deciding she hadn't
enough information to unravel the tangle of her
thoughts. Instead she smiled brightly as Katy cried
'Papa!' and hurled herself at her father.

There was another thing as well—nothing he'd said
had prepared her for a child as old as Katy—she stole
a glance at the girl, hanging on Demetrios' arm and
chattering nineteen to the dozen. Hester had somehow
arrived at the idea that her new stepdaughter was
about six years old but Katy, for all her small bones
and delicate build, was older than that—much older.
Hester decided perhaps twelve or even a bit more,
anyway, a teenager, not the child she had been
expecting. A child would have been easier, teenagers
were always an unknown quantity, and for Katy to be
that old, it meant Demetrios had been very young—
in his very early twenties—when she had been
conceived—a youthful affair with his 'distant cousin'?
Oh hell! What did it matter to her, Hester—a hundred
steep stone steps had robbed her of any desire to
indulge in mental gymnastics. . . .

Demetrios' voice interrupted her dismal thoughts.
'And Katy, this is Hester, she's not a governess like
Miss Mungo—we're married.'

Hester interrupted quickly, cursing the bumbling
heavy-footedness of men.

'Hullo, Katy,' she gave the girl a quiet smile. 'Like your papa says, we're married, but you don't have to call me Mama, not if you don't want to.' She dredged around in her memory and remembered Mia. 'I knew a little girl about your age once, she always called me "Hes". I thought we could start off by just being friends, and isn't it a good thing you speak English, because I'm hopeless at languages—I only know two words of Greek.'

Katy beamed. 'Miss Mungo taught me,' she said with a definite Scottish accent. 'She said I was a wizard at languages. I can speak French and Italian as well. When I grow up, I'm going to work for the United Nations as an interpreter.' She took a step backwards and adopted a very grown-up manner. 'Lunch won't be ready for about half an hour, would you care to partake of some refreshment now?'

Hester concealed a smile. Miss Mungo, whoever and wherever she was, had tutored her pupil very well. 'How nice,' she answered gravely and formally. 'It's been a very hot and strenuous journey from the boat, and a cup of tea would be delightful.'

'How old is Katy?' Hester and Demetrios were alone, the sun had gone down and shadows had swiftly fallen, and Katy was in her bed cuddling a well-worn koala bear whose bedraggled fur testified to many years of use. 'I had this mad idea that she was about six or seven.'

'She's nearly thirteen.' Demetrios leaned back comfortably, cradling a cup of black Turkish coffee in his hands. He sipped it thoughtfully. 'She was born when I was a little more than twenty one, a very raw young man.' He lifted his nose disdainfully. 'Had she been the age you thought, none of this would have happened, the man would have been at an age to realise that bringing a child into the world entailed some responsibilities.'

Hester moved uncomfortably and changed the subject—she didn't want a blow-by-blow account of his love affair with Athene—he mightn't mention the girl's name, but every time he said 'she', Hester would know who he was talking about. A 'very raw young man', indeed! She didn't, she couldn't, she wouldn't believe that; he'd been born with a fatal kind of charisma, guaranteed to undermine any girl's morals and get him his own way.

'Katy's going to need a whole new wardrobe,' she remarked surlily. 'I've had a look at her clothes and although it's all very good, there's not much that's suitable for an English winter.'

'Changing the subject?' Demetrios shook his head in mock reproof. 'How you do love to wriggle out of things, my Hester! I wouldn't have thought you'd suddenly shy away from the subject of a child born out of wedlock. If I remember rightly, you were very hot and went on quite lengthily about the subject one night when we were eating out.'

'And I don't much care for your island either.' She ignored him and what he said. 'It's—it's infertile, and as for this abode—I can't call it a house,'—she recalled her very brief examination of what had been the sleeping quarters in the monastery, a long line of little cells, unlit except for the pierced arches high up in the wall that separated them from the corridor, 'it reminds me of those places where they keep battery hens.' Her lips quirked as she visualised the corridor itself. Rows of wooden doors on one side and on the other, tiny windows set high in the outer wall with pictures of saints, bishops and other holy men painted like a frieze the whole length of the wall. 'Something to look at while they were meditating,' she murmured, 'but precious little comfort. Thank heaven you don't expect me to sleep down there, I'd go mad in the night!' She paused as a frightening thought struck her. 'You're not thinking of asking me to live here with Katy, are you? It'd be like being walled up alive!'

'Something you wouldn't endure, even for money?' Demetrios lit a long, thin cigar and peered at her through a cloud of blue smoke.

'Here we go again!' she sighed disgustedly.

'No, it's not "here we go again",' he almost snarled at her. 'But I'm afraid you'll have to spend a few days here, alone with Katy. I've a few things to straighten out in the hotel in Rhodes—I'll do it more quickly on my own—I haven't time to take you round sight-seeing. . . .'

'Nobody asked you to,' Hester interrupted fiercely. 'Personally, I'll be glad of the privacy. How are you getting to Rhodes—you're not going in that fishing boat, I hope?'

'No.' Demetrios set down his coffee cup and stood up. 'There's a boat coming for me tomorrow morning, a perfectly adequate cabin cruiser. That's why I couldn't spare the time for you to look around Athens. So, as I'll need to be up early, shall we go to bed?'

'To sleep, perchance to dream,' she quoted sardonically. 'Dream that this is all a dream and that one day I'll wake up to a world where everything's sane and sensible and *you* don't exist.'

'But that's the dream,' she thought he was laughing at her. 'This, my adorable wife, this is reality.'

'How nicely you put it!' she glared at him in the dimness of the room. 'Myself, I'd say this was a nightmare. I've a good mind to pray very hard to all those painted saints and bishops to have you exorcised!'

'They wouldn't do it.' He looked serious, but a small smile flickered round his well cut mouth and his heavy lids drooped so that his eyes were almost hidden and she couldn't tell whether the gleam in them was sardonic or not. 'They—those ancient churchmen—agreed wholeheartedly with the married state for the laity—they practically insisted on as many children as possible—fruits of the union which swelled the ranks of the army of God.'

'And speaking of children,' her own eyes sparkled as she took up the verbal battle, speaking calmly and judiciously. 'Have you given any thought to the matter of genes and chromosomes? I have, and I'm appalled at the evidence. I've been thinking about it a lot—it's very important, this genetic factor thing. . . .'

'And where has all this thought taken you, have you arrived at anything positive?' he queried. 'You can't have read much on the subject, not as it applies to us—you haven't had time.'

'Only that, for the best results, you should have chosen somebody else.' She looked up at him, making her face serious and her eyes glow with a candid light. 'I'll leave you out of the calculations, because although I supect you've fathered one child, a daughter, I consider the evidence to be incomplete, so I'm just working on my side of the family. My mother was an only child, a girl, and I'm also an only child, female. That's not a good track record for a man who wants a son!'

When she had finished, Demetrios was laughing uproariously, but whether it was at what she'd said or the way she'd said it, she didn't know. He seemed to be fighting for control over his amusement, and when his voice steadied, he answered her in the same clinical way that she had used.

'Then we shall just have to try, try and try again.' If it was supposed to comfort her, if failed lamentably. 'We've at least ten, possibly as many as fourteen years before you're too old to bear more children. We're almost bound to strike it lucky some time! And if we don't, think how much happiness we'll get from a really big family—and it won't be all that much hard work. You'll have Katy to help with the first two or three, and after that, the older ones will help with the babies. You look a bit stunned, my darling—don't you like the idea?'

'Ooh!' Hester squealed on a high note of indignation, and hurried past him out of the room, fumbling her way through the darkened maze of the place to find the bedroom, where she stumbled about in the dark.

Demetrios followed her, his hand touched a switch and the room sprang into light. For a moment, it meant nothing to her—one flicked a switch, light came—there was nothing marvellous about that, but—here on this lonely, barren rock of an island—miles from anywhere! Her mouth dropped open in surprise.

'A generator.' Demetrios followed the workings of her mind as though it was all written large on a blackboard as she looked around at more painted saints and bishops whose Byzantine faces and Eastern eyes watched her from the wood-panelled walls. 'It runs the lights, a large freezer, the fridge and a radio transmitter. If you want me while I'm away, Katy will show you how to use it.'

Hester hardly heard him, her fascinated gaze was on the pictures, the colours of the robes, faded by time but the gold of crowns and haloes glimmering as if newly painted.

'Don't be shy of them.' He drew her towards him and started to unfasten the buttons on her shirtwaister, smoothing the soft cotton stuff from her shoulders. 'They were a very understanding lot of men, well aware of human frailty.'

'Please!' she muttered, her eyes agonised and her hands fluttering ineffectually as she tried to push his away.

'But it'll be better this time,' he promised soothingly. 'You'll enjoy it.'

'Y-you come with a gold-plated guarantee?' Even at this stage, when she was trembling with embarrassment, she could still drag out a tart riposte.

'There's nothing plated about it,' he assured her. 'Twenty-four-carat and solid all the way through! No, don't try to hide yourself from me.' He pulled his hands away from where they were vainly trying to cover her breasts. 'I'm your husband, remember, I have the right.'

Some time during the night, Hester started a dream that turned into a nightmare, a senseless thing connected with the painted faces on the wall, and it set her bolt upright in bed, her mouth parted in a frightened scream. Demetrios stirred beside her.

'Something wrong?'

'No.' She fought her way back to reality, wiping her wet palms on the sheet 'A nightmare, something I've eaten, I expect or all that olive oil—the Russian salad was swimming in it.'

'You feel sick?'

'No again.' She slumped back on her pillows and closed her eyes determinedly. 'And if I did,' she muttered savagely, almost to herself, 'there's no need for you to put the flag up, we've only been married three days!'

He switched on the bedside light, took a look at her face and switched it off again to pull her close to him and he laughed as she slapped at his hands. 'Never mind, sweetheart, tomorrow you can organise the cooking yourself—it'll help to pass the time until I return.'

CHAPTER SIX

'How long will you be away?' Hester pushed her chair back from the table and watched her husband dunk another roll in his coffee. They had been up early, but not as early as the Greek woman, Anna, who seemed to be the chief and only head cook and bottle washer. The rolls they were eating were of her baking, and from the warmth and crispness of them, they were fresh that morning.

'You're afraid to be left here on your own?' Demetrios shook his head. 'I thought you'd appreciate the solitude, and you'll have Katy for company. You and she can get to know each other, you'll do that better if I'm not here.'

Hester gave a grunt of discontent. 'The plumbing's archaic,' she complained, 'and the water supply's niggardly. I wouldn't have liked to be here when the monastery was fully occupied—the whole place must have stunk of unwashed bodies! It's not my idea of a holiday villa.'

'Did I promise you that?' He raised his eyebrows and the lift of his lip was disdainful.

'How the hell should I know?' Hester snapped savagely. 'I can't recall what you promised. . . .'

'Twenty thousand pounds, a wedding ring and a life free from monetary worries,' he reminded her. There was a chill in his voice—the man who had teased her last night had vanished.

'And for that, you could have had the best,' she snapped, 'so why make do with me? Oh hell, I'm fed up with being a pawn on a chessboard, moved from square to square as though I'd no mind or will of my own! You never tell me anything—any bit of information I've had from you, I've had to dig out with a chisel.' She harked back to a grievance, one she had almost forgotten. 'You could have married your "distant cousin", the one I met in the hotel—the one called Athene. From her behaviour, I should have said she was slightly more than willing to fill the empty niche in your life.'

'What do you want me to say?' Demetrios leaned back lazily in his chair and looked at her through half shut eyes that gave nothing away. 'That I fancied you, or perhaps that I thought you'd suit my purpose better? Choose whichever reason you like! You *do* suit my purpose, and when you've got over your desire to be the richest woman in the world without working for it. . . .'

'Ha!' she interrupted. 'We're back to that again, are we? I'm surprised you trust me here alone with your daughter. . . . As a matter of fact, I'm surprised you trust me at all!'

'There are times when I surprise myself,' the humour crept back into his eyes, 'but you'll have to get out of this habit of being bad-tempered in the morning. You should try for a good night's sleep!' His fingers on her lips controlled her howl of wrath as Katy came bouncing into the room.

'The boat's coming!' she announced excitedly. 'May we come down to the landing with you, Papa?'

'Ask Hester,' he grinned. 'I don't think your new stepmama likes the thought of coming back up. Yesterday she said "Never again!"'

Hester chose to be contrary. 'Of course we will,' she announced firmly. 'It's just what I need, a spot of mountaineering. It'll set me up for the day,' she glanced down at her cotton trousers and flat, comfortable sandals, 'and I'm dressed for it!'

During the next two days, Hester learned about Katy and was pleasantly surprised by what she found. The child was happy without being boisterous. Apart from her ability with languages, she was pleasantly average—Hester was in no mood to cope with a budding genius—and Katy was very well behaved although a trifle old-fashioned.

Hester put this down to the effect of Miss Mungo, with whom Katy had lived for the past three years and who had been called back to Scotland less than a month ago to care for an invalid mother. Of course, Katy had desires, the main ones being to live in a house and go to a proper school with other girls.

'We've always lived in the hotels, you see,' Katy sighed tragically, 'and Miss Mungo said it's no place for a growing girl and I should meet people of my own age.' Miss Mungo had apparently said a number of things and Hester couldn't fault any of them. 'I'd like to have a dog and wear school uniform.'

'I believe your papa has a few plans in that direction.' Hester watched a smile light Katy's dark eyes. 'I'm almost sure there'll be a house, and a school. As for a dog,' she grinned, 'a house isn't a house without one!' And she left the child deep in a book of dogs, scrutinising breeds in order that the dog should be exactly right and just what was wanted.

Meanwhile, Hester wandered out into the courtyard, hoisted herself up on to the wall and peered out to sea. Over to her left loomed the dark shadow of Naxos, nearly on the skyline; Rhodes was much farther away, and she wondered what Demetrios was doing—was he stuck in an office with a desktop computer and a set of ledgers or was he decorating the side of the hotel swimming pool? Knowing Demetrios, it would be the former, and yet—she became practical—she didn't *know* Demetrios; he was merely her husband and that didn't mean she knew him.

He was the most aggravating creature, one she couldn't pin down, alternating as he did between the complete male chauvinist, a satyr and a puckish faun who teased unmercifully. He ought to be labelled, she decided drearily, 'I am a male chauvinist pig' or 'this is my humorous side'; perhaps then she'd know how to treat him! But something would have to be done about their relationship, and that soon. She was fighting for self-preservation—not to become a cypher, to retain her individuality. . . . Maybe that was what was wrong, perhaps she should just slump, give the appearance of acquiescence—be boring. It was worth a try!

Demetrios returned to the island at half past seven on Monday evening. Katy, who had spent the greater part of the day with her eye glued to the telescope which was mounted on the wall of the courtyard, came rushing in with the news.

'Papa's coming back, I can see the boat! He should be here in half an hour.'

'Big deal,' Hester said gloomily. In an effort not to think about the future, she had decided to read, but the only books were those belonging to her new stepdaughter—specially chosen, she guessed, by Miss Mungo with the aim of improving both Katy's mind and her knowledge of Scotland. Hester had dipped into *Redgauntlet* and swiftly withdrawn to seek for something a bit less convoluted and verbose. *Kidnapped* was to hand, and she sighed with relief. Robert Louis Stevenson was easier to read, but she couldn't keep her mind on it. Images of Flo, Mia and

Vilma constantly came to mind, but as soon as she concentrated on one or the other of them, they turned into Demetrios. . . .

'I'm going down to the landing to meet Papa!' That was Katy, almost dancing with excitement, and Hester thought she could understand that. After two days on this rock, a visit from the arch-fiend himself would have been welcome, if only to break the monotony. 'Are you coming with me?' Katy sounded anxious as though she thought the welcoming committee should be as large as possible. Hester closed *Kidnapped*, set it down on the table with a thump and rose to her feet.

'I'm dressed for the part,' she indicated her tee-shirt and trousers. 'But don't blame me if somebody has to send for that donkey to get me back here!'

Katy laughed aloud at the thought of somebody not wanting to climb six hundred steps, and when, on the way down, Hester made a bright comment about how fortunate it was that somebody had installed a handrail over the worst bits, the child nodded sagely.

'It was for the old men in the monastery. They were all old at the end, you know. Miss Mungo said they were hermits and then people didn't want to be hermits any more, so when the very old ones died, no new ones came.'

'That's reasonable and quite understandable.' Hester tempered her grimness with a smile and went on down, each step jolting her, but at the bottom, they went down the few steps from the landing, sat down and took off their sandals. She dipped her hot feet into the cool water with a feeling of bliss, wishing she had brought a swimsuit. There was a skimpy bikini in her case, but for some inexplicable reason she felt shy of wearing it. It didn't seem to go with monasteries!

From where they were sitting they could see the cabin cruiser, only a faint white speck in the distance to start with, but as it drew nearer they could make out the bow wave and the creamy wake of it, together with the two dark blobs which were Demetrios and the pilot. Hester scrambled to her feet and wiping them on her handkerchief, put her sandals back on. That was something else it was hard to explain, this desire to be fully clothed, even shod, when she was with Demetrios—a sort of armour? Perhaps!

The white boat came alongside the landing slowly and Demetrios, with a lithe leap, jumped ashore and Hester, watching as Katy hurled herself on her father, approved of him, in fact she felt a little curl of excitement deep in the pit of her stomach. He certainly looked good, the sort of man any right-minded girl would be glad to be married to—for sheer, animal magnificence, she awarded him top marks.

The wind had whipped his normally smoothly dressed hair into curls, his thin cotton open-necked white shirt, the sleeves rolled up to his elbows, made his olive skin look dark and satiny, and the pants he was wearing, thin dark blue ones, clung to his hips and thighs as though he'd been poured into them, and his face as he bent over his young daughter was full of laughter and gentleness.

Hester's own face grew shadowed as she straightened out the soft line of her mouth and masked the admiration in her eyes behind the fringe of her lashes. That way lay madness—she would become personally involved—she would be a pushover and it would all end in more hurt than she could take.

Determinedly she painted a bright smile on her face—remembering that Vilma had said she would get hurt; but the thing was not to let it show, so that when it came her turn to be greeted, she was cool, self-contained and strictly practical.

'Did you by any chance bring some milk back with you?' she murmured as soon as his arms closed about her. She made no attempt to evade the embrace—Katy was watching, and what her new stepdaughter thought was important to her; Katy must find everything normal.

'Milk?' Demetrios stopped with his mouth less than an inch away from hers, she could feel the warmth of his breath on her lips. 'I've been away for two days and you ask me about milk?'

'Mmm.' She stood quietly in the curve of his arm, raising clear, cool eyes to his. 'First things first, that's what I was taught. Olive oil I can take in small quantities, but goat's milk, no! And it's either that or the dried stuff reconstituted.' She turned her head slightly at the critical moment and his mouth brushed her cheek. 'If I ever come here again,' she continued serenely, 'I shall bring my own cow!'

They arrived back at Heathrow to find the English summer was behaving normally; it was raining. It had been another rushed journey. Hester felt as though her feet hadn't touched the ground since they had arrived at Piraeus, and she leaned back thankfully against the squabs of the car which had come to meet them and take them straight to the hotel. The shortest distance between two points, she mused, was a straight line, and Demetrios evidently moved only in straight lines.

'I thought we were going to have a house.' That was Katy being a bit disappointed as she looked around the immaculate suite. 'Somewhere I could have a dog.'

'I'm sure we will,' Hester consoled as she unpacked Katy's suitcases and began to hang things away in the wardrobe. 'But finding the right house takes time. Your papa will arrange it.' If there was a slight note of bitterness in her voice, Katy didn't notice. 'He's very good at arranging things.'

Demetrios didn't work in the hotel. 'Work,' he murmured as he slid reluctantly out of bed, 'and I'm a bit late. Ring down and have breakfast sent up, like a good girl.'

'Ring yourself,' Hester muttered as she rolled over and buried her head in the pillows. 'This last week's been like being on a very fast merry-go-round! Everything's been a blur until it was time to get off and hey presto, we were right back where we started. I'm suffering from jet-lag. Where are you going anyway?'

'To the offices.' A well-aimed slap connected with her rear and jerked her into life. 'I can't work here, there are no facilities and too many distractions.'

'You need facilities?' She raised her eyebrows and pushed her hair out of her eyes. 'I thought all you tycoons snoozed in your padded chairs until lunchtime and played golf all afternoon.' While she said it, her mind was busy. In his absence, she could ring Crispin's to see if there was a message from Mia. Her foster-sister would have returned from Switzerland by now—they might even be able to arrange a meeting if Mia was on night duty or had a split shift—but there was Katy. She sighed. Problems, problems! Nothing was clean and clear-cut any more.

Demetrios took the sigh to mean disappointment. 'Sorry, sweetheart—I'll meet you for lunch, that place off Shaftesbury Avenue where we first ate. You and Katy take a taxi and I'll book a table for half-past one.'

Hester was disgruntled. She took a quick shower

and dressed before breakfast arrived and contemplated, without enthusiasm, a morning with nothing to do except help Katy with the enormous jigsaw puzzle they had bought in the duty-free shop at the airport. Never before in her life—except when she had been on holiday, but that was different—had she been idle. Flo had always found work for idle hands—bedmaking, dusting, polishing, washing up and as a last resort, scrubbing something, but here—Hester gazed around the immaculate rooms and heaved a sigh of despair. There was nothing here, not even a decent book to read, unless she went back to Katy's store of Scottish period pieces.

Demetrios picked up her discontent. 'Try shopping,' he advised, holding out his coffee cup for a refill. 'That's what most women seem to do when they find time hanging heavy. You can spend some of your ill-gotten gains. . . .'

'Hard-earned money,' she corrected, 'and when I think of it—do you realise what it works out at? You mentioned a period of ten to fourteen years—that's only just over a thousand a year. I think you've bought me cheap, considering most of it wasn't your money anyway.'

'Put like that,' he smiled at her mockingly over the rim of his cup, 'you've got right on your side.' He drew out his wallet and selected a small sheaf of notes. 'Buy what you want, and there's some small change for taxis and the odd coffee and cake.'

'Thanks,' she muttered ungraciously, then suffered his parting kiss, ordered a fresh breakfast for Katy and went to wake the child. Katy blinked and then came wide awake at once, disappointed because her father had left before she had had a chance to see or speak to him.

'I wanted to ask him about the house.' She overcame her disappointment with an effort.

'We're meeting him for lunch,' Hester comforted, 'after we've done a bit of shopping.' She rattled through the hangers in the wardrobe. Katy's clothes were good, plain and utterly unexciting. 'You need a few extra things, some warmer stuff for a start. It's colder here and we don't want you going down with a chill.'

While Katy was having her breakfast, Hester went into the bedroom and made her telephone call from the bedside extension, her fingers drumming on the top of the cabinet as the other end rang and rang. It was Saturday morning, a busy time for Crispins, but surely . . . The ringing stopped and she heard a quiet, 'Crispins', at last and breathed a sigh of relief.

'It's Hester,' she announced. 'Have you had any messages for me?'

'Hester!' the receptionist squeaked with pleasure. 'Oh, it's nice to hear from you, we all thought you'd forgotten us or gone toffee-nosed—not being invited to the wedding, I mean. . . .'

'Messages,' Hester interrupted sternly. 'First things first and then we can have a gossip—but not too long, mind. You know how Crispin goes on about private phone calls.'

'You haven't changed a bit,' the receptionist giggled, 'and yes, I took a message for you yesterday, from your sister. Hang on a moment while I look it up in my private book.' There was a rustle of paper and then, 'Oh yes, here it is, let's see if I can read my own writing—your sister—she said to tell you everything's all right so far and she's back in London, so will you either write, or phone the hospital. She's on Men's Surgical, but she's starting nights next week.'

Hester felt delirious with relief. At the back of her mind, all through the last week, had been the fear that Flo wouldn't stand the journey, that something dreadful would have happened to her, and to know that everything was all right was like seeing the sun come out on a rainy day. 'Thank God,' she almost whispered it to herself.

'What's that you said?' came the disembodied voice in the earpiece. 'When are you coming round here? we're all dying to see you, and we've tipped up for a smashing wedding present—it's here, under the counter, and the silver ribbons are getting very tatty waiting for you. We've cut your picture out of the paper and we're all as jealous as hell. He looks a fab man!'

'Calm down!' Hester chuckled. Now that she knew Flo was all right, she felt like laughing aloud. 'I shall ring and make an appointment,' she said importantly with the laugh trickling through the words, 'and I shall expect the very best, mind you, I don't expect to be fobbed off with a junior.'

'Full treatment,' she was promised, 'and a facial as well, plus a couple of bottles of fizz. We'll make it a celebration. Oh lord, I'd better hang up, there's a dowager decending on me! 'Bye for now.'

'Goodbye,' Hester squeezed it in as the connection was broken, and went back to Katy feeling strangely lonely. They'd all been nice girls at Crispins and she missed the cheerful chatter, the gossip and—she searched for what it was—the relaxed atmosphere. That was it, she hadn't been relaxed since she'd met Demetrios!

And what chance had she of relaxing now? There was the visit to Mia to be planned and schemed because it was going to be awkward. She didn't want

to take Katy, and yet she couldn't bring herself to
leave the child alone in the hotel, but it all turned out
to be much easier than she had expected or hoped. On
the third day of house-hunting, Hester cried off.

'I've looked at houses for two whole days,' she
protested over the breakfast table, 'and all I can say is
that estate agents wear rose-tinted specs permanently
and they're given to gross exaggeration as well. That
place in Kingston,' she sniffed disparagingly. 'It
would have made a splendid orphanage or even a small
barracks, but nobody could ever have turned it into a
home, and the converted tithe barn near Cheam still
had the original woodworms, thousands of them. I
could hear them munching away as we were walking
round the place, their little jaws were working over-
time. You and Katy go,' she suggested. 'Find
somewhere nice and surprise me.'

Demetrios' dark eyes looked at her thoughtfully.
'And you—what are you going to do?'

'I shall have a lovely, lazy day.' Her smile glinted
with satisfaction. 'I'll start off with a hot, deep bath,
wash my hair, give myself a manicure,' she looked at
her hands ruefully. 'My nails are still recovering from
a week on your island, and then I shall dress myself
and go out.'

'Just for a walk in the park?' Demetrios helped
himself to fresh toast and his mouth was a sardonic
curve as he spread butter.

'No,' she said promptly. 'I'll do a bit of window-
shopping, I might even be tempted to buy one or two
things. . . .'

'A necklace of gold leaves, perhaps?' Demetrios
raised a dark eyebrow.

'No, again!' She smiled at him sweetly. 'I told you,
that was irreplaceable, a new one wouldn't be the

same—it wouldn't have the same memories for me. I'll buy some new stuff for my face, perhaps a new bottle of perfume, some tights. . . .'

'Nothing too expensive, then?' Hester watched his mouth curve into a smile. 'You're not going to go mad and spend some of your ill-gotten gains?'

In the circumstances, Hester thought she controlled herself very well. She didn't throw her knife on the floor and she didn't throw the coffee pot at him—instead, she sat quite still with a beautiful smile on her face, although she could feel the hair rising on the back of her neck. She flicked a glance at Katy, who was immersed in toast and marmalade, her large dark eyes slightly glazed as she thought of houses, schools and dogs, and kept the smile going as her eyes met her husband's across the table.

'No,' she replied 'That seems to be my favourite word, doesn't it? I told you, I don't have that money any more. I've donated it to a worthy cause.'

'Part shares in a hairdressing salon?' He passed his coffee cup across for a refill and as she took it, their fingers met, his closing over hers. She gave a slight shake of her head, her eyes never leaving his face.

'Not your business,' she said softly. 'And you seem to have a one-track mind, you should try lateral thinking and get out of the rut. You'll find it gives you a whole new approach—and speaking of new approaches, do you think I should have elocution lessons? Vilma suggested them for me.'

'When was that?' Demetrios was frowning slightly. 'I can't recall her saying it.'

'Didn't I tell you?' Hester put on a surprised look. 'I thought I did. She came to Crispins for a hairdo a few days before we were married—she asked for me specially.'

'And?'

'And I received the gypsy's warning, straight from the horse's mouth,' she chuckled at her own disregard of metaphors. 'I was given your ancestry and character right down to the last comma and full stop—it nearly frightened me to death, and then Vilma suggested that for a successful entrée into polite society, I really needed elocution lessons. Apparently my accent is redolent of Wapping Old Stairs.'

'Nonsense!' His eyes glinted. 'And you weren't frightened.'

'That's all you know.' She refilled his cup and passed it back to him. 'But as you've always thought, there's not much I wouldn't do for money, especially if it's in a good cause, like the advancement of plain Hester Marsh to the dizzy heights of being Mrs Demetrios Thalassis and all that entails.'

Katy had finished her toast and come back to earth, she was hearing things. 'But you're not plain, Hes. I think you're beautiful. Shall I wear my knickerbockers today—you don't think I look funny in them?'

'You look adorable in them.' Hester boosted her confidence like mad and received a sticky kiss of gratitude. 'And wash your face before you change,' she added. 'You're covered in marmalade.'

'You'll make a splendid mother,' Demetrios said admiringly, and Hester couldn't be sure if the admiration was real or assumed, so she decided to give him the benefit of the doubt—to be generous.

'It's a matter of practice,' she said lightly, and nearly went on to tell him how it had been when Flo was working and she had had to take charge of Mia, who had been small, pale and very dependant. Just in time, she stopped herself. It might sound like an appeal for sympathy, just as to tell him about Flo's illness—the reason why she had outrageously black-mailed her own mother—would be utterly mad!

It was much better that Demetrios continued to think of her as a hard-hearted, money-grubbing, semi-criminal. At least, it meant that her weak spot was covered from him so that he couldn't take advantage of it. She stole a glance at him beneath her lashes—did she love him? She didn't know. Certainly she enjoyed being married to him—well, some parts of it . . . and then Katy came back into the room in black corduroy knickerbockers, a white cotton, very frilly blouse and a dark red cardigan, looking so like a miniature Athene that Hester's heart dropped right down to the soles of her indoor slippers.

'No chance, my girl,' she told herself grimly, 'so stop getting maudlin and sickeningly sentimental.' This was just a job. Marry a man, produce a baby, a boy and then, ta-ta! A job like any other job, do it well, earn her keep. If she kept looking at it that way, she wouldn't be shattered when it all came to an end.

'What have you lined up for today?' She was determinedly bright. 'More mouldering mausoleums?'

'Cheam and Esher.' Demetrios flicked through literature from the estate agency in search of photographs and it gave her time to get her thoughts into order.

'Esher would be ideal.' Katy had come to stand beside her and she put an arm round the narrow shoulders and smiled down into the lovely little face. 'There's a very good girls' school close by, so, providing it wasn't too far for your papa to commute—or perhaps he'd prefer to stay here from Monday till Friday and just come down at weekends. . . .'

Katy grimaced and Demetrios made a disgusted noise in his throat.

'A very barren sort of marriage,' he snorted distastefully, and shook his head. 'It wouldn't be satisfactory or satisfy—either of us.' A smile glinted in his eyes and curved his mouth as he dared Hester to contradict. 'If the house in Esher is any good. . . .'

'And there's room for my dog,' Katy interrupted.

'Yes, I know.' He rumpled her hair and tugged at the ponytail. 'You're only thinking of a dog and a school, you wouldn't care if Hester and I had to sleep in a pigsty.'

Hester peered over his shoulder at the description and photograph of the Esher house. 'It can't be a pigsty, not at that price,' she protested, 'and it looks quite nice—not too big, but the price! Perhaps you'd better look for something smaller. . . .'

'Come with us and see for yourself,' he suggested mildly, but she shook her head. In addition to the things she had listed, she also intended to call on Mia, who would be getting up at about three in the afternoon. Hester had some explaining to do and the longer she put it off, the harder it would be.

'No,' she made it firm and definite. 'I'm having a day off.'

With a sigh, he produced the inevitable roll of money. 'Then buy yourself something pretty to wear and we'll have dinner out tonight. I'll have them send up one of the maids to sit with Katy.'

When they had gone, and with her mouth still warm from his parting kiss to which she had responded in a shameless manner, she made her way to the bathroom, passing the cluttered breakfast table guiltily. It was very pleasant to be able to ignore such things, to know that when she emerged from her bath everything would be cleared away, the rooms would have been cleaned and tidied and the bedlinen changed without any effort on her part, but it wasn't the sort of life she would want to lead for any length of time, it would be too boring.

A faint thought flickered through her mind—she wondered how long it would take to become pregnant. She banished the thought as swiftly as it had arisen. That would lead to all sorts of complications and she didn't want to think about them yet. Instead, she would concentrate on restoring some of the grooming which she had lost during her stay on the island.

CHAPTER SEVEN

NOTHING had changed in the Poplar flat; Hester knew that, although suddenly, as she had walked in, it seemed smaller, cramped and dingy. She scolded herself—it was nothing of the sort, just as it had always been, it was just that she had become accustomed, in a very short time, to more spacious and luxurious surroundings, and with a wry grin at herself, she hoped that this effect wasn't a lasting one, because she'd have to grow out of it some time.

In the kitchen, she filled the kettle and lit the stove before creeping along the passage to Mia's bedroom where her foster-sister was snoring delicately, her head under the bedclothes. She didn't go into Flo's room, it would be empty, the bed stripped and the wardrobe and drawers cleared, but while she didn't see that emptiness, she could pretend Flo was out shopping or perhaps gossiping with a neighbour—that she'd be home soon and she wasn't in Switzerland fighting for her life.

Back in the kitchen, she spooned instant coffee into a mug, added boiling water, two teaspoonsful of sugar and the top of the milk before carrying it in to Mia.

'Hi,' she said softly, and waited for her sister to emerge.

Mia stirred, pushing the bedclothes from her face, blinking owlishly and holding out a hand into which Hester thrust the coffee mug.

'Whatimeisit?' A yawn slurred the words and Mia

tried to focus on the bedside clock. 'Oh lord, not already! I've only been asleep ten minutes, I swear. That woman upstairs has been nailing down her carpets, that's what it sounded like.' Suddenly she sat bolt upright in bed, slopping coffee over the sheet. 'Hes! What are you doing here? I thought it was. . . .'

'Take your time.' Hester mopped up with a couple of tissues. 'Wake up properly.'

'I *am* awake,' Mia grew wrathful, 'and I've got a bone to pick with you. . . .'

'Like I said, take your time,' Hester patted Mia's thin shoulder. 'Drink your coffee, have a shower to wake you up properly and come to the kitchen, I'll make a pot of tea. Your bone won't go away and neither shall I until you've had a chance to pick it clean.'

'But I just don't understand.' Mia, freshly showered, wrapped up in a woolly gown and with her hair wound on to rollers, sat down at the kitchen table with a thump. 'I'm as mad as hell, Hes—you lied to me!'

'No,' Hester shook her head as she poured out the tea, 'I didn't lie, not exactly. I just didn't tell the truth, not all of it.'

'But to let me find out this way!' Mia dived in the pocket of her gown and produced a piece of newspaper, liberally stained with grease. 'One of the porters brought me this, he said I might find it interesting. He'd had his fish and chips wrapped up in it—or perhaps it wasn't *his* fish and chips. I bet it was that nursing aide, she's always nipping into the linen cupboard for a snack.'

'Sounds very reprehensible!'

'Stop it, Hes—it's nothing to make a joke about. How would you like it if somebody brought you a newspaper cutting about me doing something you didn't know anything about? Oh hell! I'm getting so muddled—But it doesn't alter the facts. You waited till Flo and I were safely out of the country and then you got married. . . .'

'Would Flo have gone if she'd known about the wedding?' Hester countered.

'You know damn well she wouldn't,' Mia snapped savagely. 'Wild horses wouldn't have got her on that plane, but of all the hole-and-corner things to do, you could at least have told me. And that's not all, is it?' She consulted the grubby cutting. 'It says here—oh damn, why couldn't whoever it was have bought something less greasy to wrap this round—I can hardly read it. It says "Mr Demetrios Thalassis". Now you explain that away, Hes.'

'Simple.'

'No, it's *not* simple, and neither am I!' Mia's voice rose to an outraged squeal. 'The last time you were here, you said there was a man, you also said he wanted to marry you. You even hinted that you might move in with him when you'd thought about it. You also said you were going away for a while to think about it some more, and that was all right with me. I didn't say a word about it to Flo, you know how she is—but did you tell me the man was some sort of relative of your mother's? No, you didn't. . . .'

'And now you know why I didn't.' Hester went across to the window where she stood watching the traffic making its way to the Blackwall Tunnel. 'Look at the fuss you're making! If I'd told you then, you'd have wanted chapter and verse, and then I'd never have got you on the plane, never mind Flo.'

'But you *knew* you were getting married!' Mia was bubbling with anger and hurt. 'You can't do something like that in five minutes—in fact, the day you put the money in the bank for me you *must* have known. What was it, Hes? Did you have the idea you were going up in the world and we wouldn't be good enough for your fancy new relations, because if that's what you thought you needn't have bothered to come here today.'

'You know it wasn't like that.' Hester remained at the window, staring out, but she could no longer see the traffic for the blur of the tears in her eyes—they were threatening to spill over and run down her cheeks, so she kept her head averted. 'Look, love, to put it simply, we made a deal. Vilma sent him. I think she was trying to frighten me off, but instead he offered to help me.'

'The damn swine!' Mia's outrage showed in her wrathful growl. 'Men!'

'Stop it,' Hester said wearily. 'You're swearing like a trooper!'

'The effect of being on Men's Surgical, you learn a lot. But you couldn't have thought you were pregnant, it would be far too soon to tell, or has all this been going on for longer than I think? Hes! There wasn't any need to marry him, even if you were. I'd have looked after you and we'd have got round Flo somehow. . . .'

Hester turned from the window at last. 'Will you let me finish?' she snarled. 'You keep interrupting when you only know half of it. He didn't seduce me and I didn't think I was having a baby. I said it was a deal. I wanted the money for Flo, Vilma was doing a denying thing, so Demetrios helped me. He wanted a stepmother for his little daughter, that's all. It was a straight swap, although I wouldn't tell him what I wanted the money for, I thought he might refuse to help. He thought I was on the make for myself, you see,' she explained tiredly. 'I didn't want to disillusion him—I *wanted* him to think I could be bought. When he made the offer, I couldn't pass it up, could I? And I couldn't tell you—look at the fuss you're making now the deed's done, and think what you'd have said if you'd known about it beforehand. I'd been to too much trouble to have the deal mucked up at the last moment.'

'Hey!' Mia crossed to stand beside her, sharp eyes taking in the trace of tears. 'Hes, you're crying! What's he done to you? Oh, I could kill him for this, I've a good mind to go and see him and scratch his eyes out!'

'You couldn't.' Hester wiped her eyes with the back of her hand and put an arm round Mia's slender waist. 'My pet, you're too little and much too gentle—see,' she lifted one of Mia's hands. 'No claws, and in any case, he hasn't done anything to me. It's just me being foolish.' She summoned up a smile. 'It's the strain, getting the money and then landing myself with a husband and a stepdaughter—I don't know if I'm on my head or my heels!'

'And worrying about Flo.' Mia squeezed the hand on hers. 'It sounds a pretty ropey marriage, is it going to work out? I think the best thing you can do is tell him about Flo straight away.'

Hester shook her head obstinately. 'Make a plea for sympathy? Try to make him see me in a better light? No!'

Mia suddenly laughed. 'Oh, Hes! I believe you're in love with the man and you want him to love you back and for yourself *alone!*' she almost sang the last words. 'Poor old hardhearted, hardbitten Hes, gone all romantic! Can't say I blame you, this photograph's nothing much, but he looks a proper dreamboat. All right, love,' as she saw tears starting again in her sister's eyes, 'do it the hard way—but remember, I'm here if things get too tough, you can cry on my shoulder any time. It's your wilful pride,' she snorted. 'Remember, Flo tanned you for it often enough and you're still not cured. You always would make life hard for yourself. Never mind, maybe you're right and the less he knows the better—he'll learn in time. How did your mother take it, the marriage, I mean?'

'Venomously!' Hester gave a watery chuckle. 'When you grow claws, my pet, there's a lady you can scratch with my blessing and approval, that's if I don't do it first myself. Let's make another pot of tea and you can tell me all about Flo.'

'It's a marvellous place.' Mia busied herself with the kettle and emptying the teapot. 'Flo was a bit dim when she arrived, but she'd pulled round a bit by the next day. It's up in the mountains, you can see for miles and she's a lovely room all to herself and a couple of English nurses who are taking turns to special her, so she's always got someone to talk to. . . .'

'We did the right thing, then,' Hester worried at it. 'Even if. . . .'

'Even if!' Mia was firm and serene. 'She's having the best, nobody could do more for her than you've done. She's waiting for letters from you and she gave me a lot of instructions, like seeing we were good girls while she was away or she'd tan our hides when she came home. . . .'

It was nearly five o'clock when Hester left the flat after a tearful goodbye to Mia and a promise to keep in touch through Crispins and the hospital phone if there was anything urgent—if not, as Mia said, letters would do.

At the end of the road she was lucky. A cruising taxi was passing and she hailed it and jumped inside almost before it had stopped. She was late, she would be late arriving back at the hotel—her chin came up aggressively and her soft mouth firmed. So what! She was entitled to some time to herself, surely? And yet, for some silly reason which she couldn't quite pinpoint, she didn't want Demetrios to be cross with her. Probably a carry-over from Vilma's nasty little hints about his character, it was strange how nasty remarks always make a deeper impression than nice ones, how they lingered on at the back of one's mind.

She counted her parcels and sighed with relief. They were all present. The dress she had bought, a rather dramatic garment in black silk—cut like a cheongsam and loaded with silver embroidery—would be rather crumpled since she had refused the cardboard box as being too cumbersome and insisted it was put in an ordinary carrier bag. But it could be hung in the bathroom while she showered so that the creases would drop out.

It had been incredibly expensive; she had gulped at the price. The filmy black underwear which she couldn't resist—and couldn't truly afford, the new pair of black evening slippers—which she badly needed, the tights, make-up and perfume—she'd paid for all of those herself and she hoped this would be her last big expense for some time to come as she had made a considerable hole in her savings.

Demetrios didn't ever seem to use money as money, to him, it was something he kept apart for small, incidental expenses. She sniffed disparagingly—that was all right for him, he had a large bank balance, but she wasn't so fortunate. Her remaining two hundred odd pounds wouldn't go far if she had to splash out like this frequently.

'Papa's bought the house in Esher!' Katy came

whooping through the lounge almost as soon as Hester opened the door. She had obviously been lying in wait, and equally obviously she was beginning to forget a great many of Miss Mungo's excellent dicta. The main one being that little girls should be seen and not heard. She flung herself on her new stepmother in an ecstasy of delight. 'It's very nice, and we drove past the school—Oh, Hes, you should see it, it's wonderful and there's a lovely place with trees where I can take my dog for a walk.'

Demetrios followed his daughter more sedately, an eyebrow cocking at the sight of the parcels. 'Something nice?'

'You paid for it.' Hester untangled herself from Katy's grip and tossed over the bag containing the dress. 'You judge for yourself. It's a bit rumpled, but the creases will soon drop out.'

'I'll ring down to reception,' Katy offered with the aplomb of somebody who had lived in hotels for most of her life. 'They'll send somebody up to take it away and press it,' and she sped off to the phone, leaving Hester and Demetrios and a small pile of even smaller parcels.

Unerringly, he pinpointed the source of her embarrassment and prised her fingers apart to peep into the bag. 'Oh!' His fingers probed and emerged with a wisp of black silk inset with lace, and he looked from it to the dress now draped over his arm. 'Very sexy!'

'If you don't approve, I'll change it for red flannel,' Hester offered sweetly. 'Everything shall be as my lord and master desires.'

'Liar!' he reproved. 'Don't put on that subservient tone with me, my girl! You're about as biddable as a tigress and you don't give a damn for what I want.

There are times when I understand you and others when I can't make you out. You know what you are, my dear? You're a mass of contradictions. Why wasn't I allowed to pay for everything. You know I've opened an account for you at Harrods?' And as she opened her eyes in surprise, 'You've left the receipt in this bag, it's marked "cash sale".'

'And you don't miss a trick,' she sniffed haughtily. 'The dress is for your benefit, you're taking me out to dinner and I have to think of your image, don't I, but what I wear underneath is my own business. What I mean is, the dress is for public display and I wouldn't like any of your acquaintances to think you'd married a frump, so I think you're entitled to pay for it. The other things are—well, private. I bought them because I either liked or needed them, so I pay for those myself.'

'And you're rich enough to do so,' he added.

'Ha!' Hester had got her second wind and was finding the verbal fencing quite exhilarating. 'You only went as far as "cash sale" on that ticket thing. Look at the price and you'll know I can't afford many things like that. I'll soon go through my savings.'

'Leaving you with only your nest egg which you've salted away somewhere,' and at her scowl of wrath, 'Never mind, darling. You keep it safe, you never know when you'll need it.'

'Pooh!' She bypassed him on the way to the bedroom. 'Why should I do that when I've got a wealthy husband?'

'Because you're complicated, contrary and contradictory.' Demetrios followed her and watched as she hung up the jacket of her suit.

'Wrong again,' she shook her head at him as she kicked off her shoes. 'I'm none of those things. You're

suffering from an overdose of vivid imagination. Take
an aspirin and lie down for half an hour, you'll soon
feel better,' and with a toss of her head, she rejoined
Katy to listen to a glowing account of the school
buildings, the conservatory attached to the house
which would be an excellent place to keep a puppy
while it was still making puddles and, last but not
least, the important question of what puppy—big or
small, hairy or smooth.

Demetrios waited till Katy had run out of questions
and Hester was mentally fatigued with answering so
many before he lounged over to join them, effectively
putting to an end the debate on what sort of dog would
be best.

'One that's small enough to be ignored, yet too
big to sleep on your bed,' he decreed, 'and also, since
Hester will have to look after it while you're in
school, it had better be a nice, well-behaved and
gentle type. Remember, if it bit Hester, she'd
probably bite back!'

Katy went into peals of laughter at the thought and
went off to her bedroom to consult the oracle—her
newly acquired book on dogs.

'That'll keep her quiet for a while,' Demetrios
remarked as the door closed behind the child. 'Now,
let's get back to our conversation and your remedy for
my over-vivid imagination. Is there a nurse in your
family, by any chance?'

Hester, who had been idly fitting in several pieces of
Katy's jigsaw, felt a warning prickle of goosepimples
down her spine. Her hand remained poised over the
small table and she appeared to be contemplating the
half-finished puzzle with rapt attention, but her mind
wasn't on it. He couldn't know! There was no way he
could have found out! She'd been very careful about

everything and super-careful about what she'd said—
so he must be making a chance remark.

'What a strange remark.' She tried a piece of the
puzzle and when it wouldn't fit anywhere, she tossed
it back in the pile. 'You know I don't have any family
except Vilma, and she's not my idea of a nurse.
Whatever gave you that idea?'

'You did, with your suggestion that I should take an
aspirin,' he chuckled. 'You sounded as though you
were quite used to coping with semi-invalids.'

'But I am.' She was on safe ground now and could
smile widely. 'Remember, I've been working with girls
ever since I was seventeen, anything between ten and
fifteen of them, and with that number, headaches are the
rule rather than the exception. If you show too much
sympathy, they'll decide the pain's too great to be borne
and they'll go home, leaving the place understaffed, so I
learned early to temper the sympathy with a brisk,
practical approach. It saved a lot of hassle.'

'Yes.' He put a finger under her chin and forced her
face round so that he could look into her eyes. He
wasn't brutal about it, she felt no pain, only a quiet,
implacable insistence. 'But the brisk practicality's only
on the surface, my dear—isn't it?'

'All the way down to the bone,' she contradicted.
'I've got few emotions and I keep them under very
strict control. Hardhearted Hester, that's me, and I
pride myself on it.' Her eyes glowed and there was a
wry twist to her mouth. 'How else could I have done
what I've done?'

'Tell me what you've done,' he invited, and she
faced him squarely, thinking up several rather
romantic versions of her activities, dismissed them
because they sounded too highfalutin' and came out
with it baldly, no punches pulled.

'I put the black on my own mother—salted away the loot where nobody will ever find it.' She thought about that for a moment and qualified it. 'No, that's not quite correct. Like I said, I donated it to a good cause and then I hopped into bed with a complete stranger—you could hardly say those were the actions of a shrinking violet, could you?' She paused thoughtfully and an impish smile lit her eyes. 'I made on that deal as well. A glorious honeymoon, sitting in an ex-monastery on a rock in the middle of the Mediterranean—I swapped my bedsit for this,' she glanced round at her lush surroundings. 'I'm going to be installed in a house in the country and used as a breeding machine and you've just bought me a very nice evening dress! How could any girl be dissatisfied with that?'

'And you've also gained a charming stepdaughter,' he pointed out, 'and you're going to be an equally charming and devoted wife.'

'Hmm,' Hester wrinkled her nose. 'I shan't cheat on you, if that's what you mean. We made a bargain and I've no intention of doing you dirt.' Once more, her eyes sparkled maliciously. 'How could I when you've given me so-o-o much!'

Fortunately, the waiter chose that moment to come in with the tea trolley, followed by a middle-aged maid who scooped up the dress and went off with it over her arm.

Hester took a last, long, considering look at herself in the full-length mirror in the bedroom and stepped back, satisfied. It was amazing what a beautiful gown did for a girl—that and a great deal of care and attention to details. She had spent a long time on her face and it had been time well spent. Her eyes looked wider, darker and mysterious, her rather firm chin now looked much more delicate and her mouth was darkly but softly red. Her hair, drawn back into a loose coil on her neck, first brushed until her scalp tingled and then polished with a silk hankie, glowed like well waxed wood. She smelled of 'Arpège' perfume, but it was the dress which was going to catch the eye. Demetrios would have no need to be ashamed of her, despite her humble beginnings.

Turning back to the mirror, she admired the way the silver embroidery caught the light, making the black of the silk even more dense, and she took a trial step so that the side slit to just above her knee parted to show her long, slender leg and one high-heeled black silk sandal. Nothing wrong there, she decided— it might have been a bit much if the dress had been décolleté, but it wasn't. It came right up to her throat, finishing in a little mandarin collar and only her arms were bare. She certainly wasn't suffering from over-exposure.

Demetrios came into the bedroom just as she was ferreting in the wardrobe for her camel coat, and the gleam of appreciation in his eyes made her blush. She covered her momentary embarrassment with a snort. 'Nobody will see this,' she threw the coat across her shoulders. 'I'll drop it off in the cloakroom as soon as we arrive. No,' as he took a pace towards her, 'I've done a lot of hard work to achieve this effect and if you start mauling me, it'll all be spoiled,' she rattled on, words falling from her lips as she went past him to the door.

'Is Katy asleep? Has the maid come up yet? I hope you'll order something substantial for dinner, I had a very scrappy lunch in a cafeteria and I didn't feel like doing justice to those cucumber sandwiches at teatime.'

She continued chatting volubly all the way down in

the lift, it was a good cover for her increased heartbeat and the breathlessness which had attacked her when Demetrios entered the bedroom. She had seen him in business clothes, in jeans and a tee-shirt, in a formal suit—he looked good in all of them, but now she was seeing him dressed to go out for the evening, which made him quite something. Had the situation between them been different, she would have gone quite starry-eyed with pride—his white shirt made his face just that little bit darker, his evening jacket fitted him as though he had been poured into it and his thin black evening trousers made his legs look as though they went on endlessly.

It was't fair, she mourned to herself. He'd no right to be so damn good-looking—he'd no right to smile at her as he was doing, as if he knew every thought running through her mind. He put up a hand to smooth his hair and instead dislodged a bit in front which immediately became a curl and flopped over his forehead, and she had to fight the desire to smooth it back with tender fingers.

The spate of words falling from her lips dried up suddenly and she had to turn her back on him and think very hard about Katy and Athene. She clenched her hands tightly round the flat black silk purse—it hadn't cost her a penny, it had come with the dress—and when the lift slowed, it was only stubborn pride which prevented her from throwing herself at Demetrios and asking to be taken back upstairs again. The whole of her was a screaming, molten mess of wanting to be made love to—she slid a glance at him through rather heavily mascaraed eyelashes and her chin lifted while her mouth tightened. He was almost smirking with triumph, damn him. He knew!

Over her shoulder, his hand came to press the

release button on the lift door. 'Would you rather not go out, Hester? We could have a quiet dinner in the suite and an early night,' he suggested.

'Not on your life!' The door slid open and she stumbled into the cold dimness of the underground garage. 'You promised me a night out and that's what I'm having. I wouldn't miss it for the world! Hurry up,' she stood by the door of the car and faked a shiver, 'it's rather cold here and I can't wait to get to the fleshpots!'

The night-club was crowded, every table seemed to be occupied, and Hester looked around with well concealed awe. There were so many beautifully dressed women, so many jewels, and she was glad she'd spent so much of Demetrios' money on this dress. She was also glad she was hungry, it would have been such a waste to come to a place like this and fiddle with a fillet of sole—hastily she consulted the menu and made her choice before she took a sip at her aperitif.

'How long will it be before we can move into the house?'

Demetrios delayed his reply while he made up his mind about food. He took so long that Hester felt her blood pressure rising. 'What are you having?' He looked at her over the top of the menu as though she hadn't asked a question.

'Fillet steak, mushrooms, asparagus and sautéed potatoes,' she answered briefly. 'I asked you a question—when are we moving into the house, or is that another big secret?' Any change in her heartbeat was now entirely due to his delaying tactics. After all, he must have made some plans, and surely she should be the first to know.

'We'll talk about it later,' he told her dismissively.

'You don't want to rush things, my dear. Haven't you learned that a good meal and some wine mellows a man?' He smiled at her mockingly. 'We should have stayed in the hotel, the food there's as good as anything here and you'd have got your own way with much less trouble—pillow talk's always more productive.'

'I am *not* trying to get my own way,' Hester denied vigorously. 'And as for what you call pillow talk,' she looked up, met his gaze and flushed, 'I wouldn't stoop to a thing like that!' Her flush died away, leaving her face pale and cold. 'No, don't tell me I sold myself once and then ask why I'm being so fussy now.' She kept her voice low and hardly moved her lips. 'You helped me once when I was desperate, but it was only once. I promised myself I'd never ask you for anything ever again, and certainly I won't make capital out of the fact that we're good together in bed.'

'But you're asking for a house. . . .'

'Not for me,' she interrupted. 'For Katy. It's what she wants and it's time she settled down to a proper life, an ordinary life where she has a home and family like other children. So, what about this house?'

'We have to allow about two months for repairs and decoration and then another few weeks to furnish it. . . .' He was being reasonable.

'Rubbish!' Hester muttered the word under her breath, but he caught the movement of her lips.

'You said?'

'I said "Rubbish".' She moved aside slightly as the waiter put avocado shells stuffed with a creamy mixture in front of her and she picked up a fork and spoon, holding them as though she was going to kill whatever was in the mixture. 'Two months for repairs and decoration in an empty house! I don't believe it, unless the damn place is falling to bits—in which case you shouldn't have bought it! How long has it been empty?'

'A few months,' he shrugged. 'The wiring will have to be checked. . . .'

'That's a day's work.' She was no longer biddable, although she managed to keep her voice down. 'Two months! I know you're a big man in your own field, but honestly. . . . What's wrong with the house that a few fires and a bit of paint won't put right? And don't glare at me as if it was all my fault!'

'You could have come with Katy and me to see it,' Demetrios reminded her gently.

'So, it *is* all my fault. I just *knew* you'd find some way to blame me,' irritably, she pushed aside the avocados which she had hardly touched. 'I might have known you'd think of some way to get back at me for taking a day off! There ought to be a union for married women, perhaps then we'd get a charter or something laying down the rules and conditions of employment.'

'You're overworked?'

'Of course not,' she muttered savagely while she kept a sweet smile going for the benefit of anybody who might be looking. 'That's the trouble, I suppose. I'm not used to an idle life and there's so little to do—by the end of next week, Katy and I will have seen all the sights—twice! Couldn't I go down there and see for myself?' Try as she would, she couldn't keep a note of desperation out of her voice, and it was reflected in her eyes. 'Some firms will tell you anything,' she heard herself almost wheedling. 'If I could see the place, I'd have a much better idea.'

'You want this house so badly?' Demetrios poured

himself a glass of wine, and raised an eyebrow at her empty glass. 'Want some?'

Hester shook her head, both at the question about the house and the wine. 'It's not that, I'm thinking of Katy. It's more than time she started to live a normal life—there's nothing wrong with the hotel, but she ought to start getting used to not being waited on hand and foot and it's all very restrictive. Please understand,' she was serious. 'In a home, a real home, she'd learn some responsibility, she'd have her own things around her and learn to care for them instead of walking away from a mess and leaving the clearing to somebody else. Oh,' she sighed exasperatedly, 'you don't even know what I'm talking about, do you, but I'm right, I know I am. Am I getting through?'

'Only in so far as if I don't give way, you'll keep hammering at me,' he chuckled, and watched as a waiter slid a plate in front of her, and when she had made her choice from the proffered dishes, 'We'll go down tomorrow, make a day of it. I'm pleased you're taking an interest at last. Tell me, are you an expert in moving house? Have you done it before?'

'Not houses—flats.' She felt much happier and in consequence her steak looked much more appetising—she cut into it and licked her lips. 'I've never lived in a house, only flats. They were very nice, of course, and we made them homey, if you see what I mean, but we always had to be careful, not run about too much because of the people in the flat below, not have the television or the radio on too loud in case we annoyed the neighbours.'

Much later, they entered the hotel suite and Demetrios watched Hester as she kicked off her sandals and sank into a chair. 'You've enjoyed yourself?'

'Like the parson's egg, it was good in parts,' she admitted cautiously. 'I wouldn't like to do it too often, it would play hell with my waistline. I'll just take a look at Katy and then I'm off to bed or I'll be dead in the morning.'

'Katy's all right,' he murmured as he drew her to her feet and slid his arms round her. 'You sound a bit disappointed. Didn't the fleshpots appeal, and will this make it any better?'

'Rounding off the evening with a peal of bells?' she enquired sarcastically.

'But I make them ring for you.' His mouth was so close she could feel his warm breath on her lips and she softened against him, almost weeping at her own weakness. There was never a word of love, yet he could lift her to the stars—it wasn't fair!

CHAPTER EIGHT

HESTER parked the Mini outside the garage and walked towards the house. Her new domain, and although there was pleasure in the thought, it was tinged with bitterness. Flo should have had somewhere like this to live, somewhere with space and a garden to tend instead of a cramped flat, a few pots of spring bulbs and a Busy Lizzie on the parlour windowsill. She wondered whether it would be possible to spring Flo on Demetrios, when and if her foster-mother ever came back from the clinic. It would be the ideal place for a long, long convalescence.

And the house would be so easy. She looked at it—a lovely, solid type place, not so old that it was in permanent danger of falling down and not so new that it hadn't gained a little dignity. She chuckled as she recalled the estate agent's description: 'Spac. det. hse. 4 bed. plus mstr bed. with shwr en suite. 2 bath. 2 recp. lnge. fit. kit. hall. cloaks. C.H. dbl.gge. Lge. garden & patio. Idcal sit for commuters'—which all added up to a lot of space when it was turned into proper English, and it hadn't taken anywhere near two months to move in.

Secretly, she was of the opinion that the threatened two months' delay had been in the nature of a firecracker which Demetrios had tied to her tail to make her show a bit of interest, and of course he had succeeded. She had come down the very next day and stormed through the house, reducing the two months to two weeks; gone with him and Katy to the school where her husband had been bland but firm so that Katy was taken, after a short examination of her mental prowess—less than seven weeks before the end of the summer term. On trial, of course, to see if she fitted in, but Hester had no doubts about that—Katy would make herself fit!

After that, they had gone back to town, ordered Katy's school uniform, which was the most important thing, and then browsed about furtniture stores in search of less essential things like chairs, beds, tables and soft furnishings. It had been a hectic two weeks, but she had enjoyed every moment of it, especially when Demetrios had presented her with the Mini. As he had pointed out, it wasn't a new one, so a few bumps wouldn't show—he had come with her on her first outing and when her nervousness had passed, he had said she was a careful driver, well suited to country roads but hopeless in town!

Hester hadn't cared about that; she wasn't going to drive in town, she was only going to take Katy to school each morning and bring her home in the evening, with perhaps a few short shopping trips thrown in for good measure.

With a feeling of pleasurable anticipation, Hester went round to the back of the house and entered by the door which led to the kitchen. Here, she unpacked the small amount of shopping she had done and made coffee for herself and the daily woman before starting on some lunch for herself. Her day was planned out right down to the last five minutes, so that when she was bringing Katy home from school, she stopped the Mini with considerable reluctance when Katy squealed excitedly:

'Did you see that, Hes? It said there were puppies for sale!'

They'd been passing the board stuck in the hedge for nearly two weeks and Hester was quite familiar with the list of commodities chalked on the black surface. Bedding plants, free range eggs, lettuce—but today there was a roughly scrawled addition, 'Puppies for sale'. She backed the Mini up and shook her head. 'I thought you'd decided on a golden cocker spaniel, and you won't get anything like that here. This isn't a registered breeding kennels.'

'At the end of that lane my puppy's waiting for me—I just know it!' Katy's eyes were glazed with hope and she was doing a credible imitation of the Delphic Oracle. 'Please, Hes!'

'Just one dog and a little bitch.' The owner of the small holding led the way to a whitewashed outhouse. 'Which do you want? The bitch'll be cheaper, of course.'

'Both!' Katey was buoyant with hope and regardless of expense.

'The dog,' Hester was more cautious. 'If it's suitable, that is.'

'Collies.' The owner seemed short of conversation, but after noticing Hester's frown when she looked at the two squirming little bundles of black and white fluff, he added, 'Welsh collies, not the Border ones. Eight weeks old—weaned and wormed—five pounds for the dog and three for the bitch, that's what I'm going to ask at the livestock auction tomorrow. They'll sell like hot cakes.'

Hester doubted the truth of that statement, but Katy was already clutching the dog pup and her small face had firmed into an adult determination.

'This is *my* dog, Hes, I told you it was waiting for me. This is the one I want—see, he knows me already.'

'And the spaniel?'

'No,' Katy shook her head, 'I don't want one of those after all, this'll be much better and he's very small. I don't expect he'll grow very big, do you?'

Hester knew nothing about dogs except what she had read in Katy's book, and to her one pup looked very like another. It certainly looked small, but it was with reluctance and a sense of foreboding that she produced a five-pound note from her purse.

At half past six that evening, Hester's well ordered kitchen was in a state of chaos, so that when Demetrios walked in, she was on her hands and knees with a floorcloth, mopping up a truly tremendous puddle, while Katy, on her hands and knees, was chasing the author of the mess. Chairs were skidding on the well polished floor tiles and Demetrios paused in the doorway, his eyebrow nearly touching his hairline as a black and white pup crawled from under the table and squirmed abjectly at his feet.

'Katy has her dog!' His lips twitched. 'What is it?'

'Heinz fifty-seven varieties, I think.' Hester finished her mopping up operation, disposed of the bucket and cloth and removed her rubber gloves.

'It's a collie,' Katy protested.

'It's a mongrel,' Hester corrected, 'and it has all the bad traits of mongrels. It has no dignity—look at the way it's making up to your papa, it's grovelling!'

'It *loves* him!' Papa's daughter was indignant. 'It's just the kind of dog we need, it won't grow too big, will it, Papa?'

Demetrios tickled the pup's white bib and stooped to examine the white paws. 'I'm sorry to disappoint you, Katy, but I'm afraid he's going to grow to be very big,' a pink tongue licked his fingers lovingly, 'and Hester's quite right—he grovels!'

'I shan't be home tomorrow night.' Dinner was over, Katy was in bed and asleep, the pup was ensconced in the bottom half of a packing case in the conservatory and Demetrios was lounging in a chair in the sitting room. 'I have to go to Athens the day after tomorrow, an early morning flight, so I'll stay in town and take a taxi to the airport.'

Hester looked up from her book on the correct care of roses. 'How long will you be away?' She didn't know whether to be glad or sorry—one part of her was singing with triumph that now she would be able to please herself what she did, where she went and who she visited, while the other part was telling her that she'd be cold and lonely, that she'd miss him.

'About two weeks, maybe a little less.' He lit a cigar with a spill from the fireplace—it was only a log fire, but the flames made the big room more cosy, more homelike. 'I shall be four or five days in Athens and then I have to visit Crete and Cyprus. Shall you miss me?' He didn't look at her but kept his eyes on the softly spluttering logs.

'No,' she replied hardily, 'I shouldn't think so. I've got plenty to do—as long as you're back for Katy's birthday, which is a fortnight today exactly.'

'You've something planned for it?'

'Only the usual party,' she explained. 'Tea and a pop session afterwards, she's invited some of her school friends and I was relying on you to ferry them home afterwards. I couldn't get them all in the Mini.' She sprang up suddenly and went to the television. 'There's a good horror film on. Do you want to see it?'

This time, Demetrios looked away from the fire, directly at her. 'I was hoping—I thought we might talk about the future.'

Some imp of perversity driving her, she switched on the TV and turned the volume up full. 'When you come back from your travels,' she had to shout over the noise. 'This is a good film, I've been looking forward to it all day—I don't want to miss it.' And she fixed her eyes firmly on the screen with all the appearance of a person bombed out of her mind by the images that flickered across it. She watched the film, the news, a short programme about the theatre, the late news and the news commentary that followed it, and then yawned prodigiously. She hadn't really heard or seen a thing, it had all been patterns on a screen and noises coming from people's mouths.

'Going to bed now. Goodnight,' she announced shortly, and crept upstairs like a ghost, failing even to look in on Katy, something which she always did.

In the bedroom, she snorted to herself. Her husband was going away for a few days and she was behaving as though all the lights in the world had gone out—if she didn't feel so damn miserable, she would have laughed herself silly. Even a hot bath didn't help; she felt just as miserable when she climbed out of it as when she'd stuck her toe in to test the water. With a sigh, she slid into bed and resolutely turned her back on where Demetrios would be sleeping, closing her eyes and almost praying for sleep to come quickly, but things never happen when you want them to, she told herself savagely as she stayed tense and wakeful, listening for a footstep on the stairs or in the corridor outside the bedroom door.

She heard the hiss of his shower and then the quiet pad of his feet across the bedroom floor and felt the depression of the bed as he slid into it. He switched on the bedside light—she could see it through the thin membrane of her eyelids, but she lay quite still, breathing evenly and deeply.

'You're not asleep, Hester.' Competently, he turned her to face him. 'What's the matter? What do you want me to say, that I'll send somebody else?

'No!' she wanted to scream it at him, and she compressed her mouth into a thin, tight line to stop the words coming out. Words she daren't say because if she did, and if he heard them, she'd be no more than a chattel, a poor, bought thing, utterly dependent on him. So how could she tell him she wanted him to say he loved her? He didn't know the meaning of the word, or, if he did, he'd never think of her that way.

'No, of course not,' she forced herself to say. 'You're a business man, I know that, and it's quite normal you should have to travel, it's part of your job. I'm only sorry I—we can't come with you. I'd like to have a second look at Athens and I've never been to Crete or Cyprus.'

'Then give me something sweet to take with me,' Demetrios murmured, pulling her closer, his hands sliding down to her hips, 'so I'll come back quickly for more.'

'I'm tired,' she protested, 'and I think I've a headache coming on, it's been a busy day.'

'Liar!' he teased. 'You're vexed because I'm leaving you for a few days. Will you miss me?'

'Like a hole in the head!' But it was her last spark of defiance as she softened against him. His mouth was on hers and she went into the sweetly familiar, dizzying spiral where her body moved sensuously against his until all the stars exploded in a triumph of consummation. 'Help me,' she prayed to some strange god. 'I'm becoming an addict, I can't live without him.'

On the morning of Katy's birthday, Hester woke feeling on top of the world. According to her last telephone call from Demetrios, he would be home this evening, so the absence of a birthday card from him caused her no concern—she was able to comfort Katy with the thought that very few children received cards from both their parents and that since there was one by the side of her breakfast plate marked as being from Papa *and* Hester, there would possibly be some extravagant present under his arm when at last he walked through the door.

Solaced by this thought, Katy went joyously to school, having first fed her pup and taken him for a walk in the garden where he had uprooted several smallish rose bushes and, driven by hunger, had eaten the plastic rose of a new watering can.

By three o'clock Hester's preparations for the party were complete. Katy had discovered that while an iced birthday cake was quite acceptable, girls of her age no longer required jelly or any other childish thing. Paper hats and a tea at half past four were also old-fashioned, and Katy had settled for barbecued beefburgers on the patio at seven with a few fairy lights strung in the small saplings that grew close by.

Hester made herself a cup of tea, took it into the lounge where the wide window looked out over the front garden, then sat down and put her feet up for the half hour or so before she needed to go to fetch Katy from school. The silence was profound, so much more restful than the noise of London traffic, and her eyes drooped shut, only to fly open a few moments later at the sound of a car turning into the drive and the crunch of wheels on the gravel surface. Without looking out of the window, she went flying to the door to fling it open, and her smile of welcome froze on her face. The car was a blue Lancia upholstered to match the speedwell blue of Vilma's silk suit and her mother was standing at the door, her hand raised to the bell push.

'Good afternoon.' Vilma stepped past her into the house without a by-your-leave. 'So good of you to see me,' she drawled. 'For one moment I thought you were going to refuse me the house.'

'As if I'd ever think of doing such a thing!' Hester retorted sardonically as she ushered Vilma into the lounge. Her mother accepted gracefully, went past her and seated herself in Hester's favourite chair.

'Oh, tea—how civilised!' Vilma touched the fat teapot with a gloved hand. 'And freshly made, so nice. Shall I pour you a cup?'

'Mine's already poured.' Hester motioned to her rapidly cooling cup. 'If you can bring yourself to wait for a few seconds, I'll fetch you a cup and saucer from the kitchen.'

When she came back, Vilma was still sitting there, smoking a cigarette and looking about her, eyes taking in every detail. Demetrios had allowed Hester to choose which pieces of furniture she wished, their shape and size, but the things he had bought were so much more luxurious than her more economical choices and Vilma was appreciating them. 'You've done very well for yourself,' she observed. 'It seems Demetrios can afford far more than I thought. Is he generous?'

'I've no fault to find with his generosity.' Hester poured tea into the fresh cup and handed it over, worrying her brow into a slight frown. Vilma looked exactly as she had done when Hester had met her before, both at Crispins and after the mockery of a wedding—slim, svelte, incredibly well groomed and

dressed and very well preserved, but today there was a
tautness about her—almost as though she was nervous.

Hester slid down into the chair—it was the one
Demetrios had bought for himself, wider and deeper
than her own and with fat pillows and a low, long seat.
It was ideal for him, he liked to sprawl with his long
legs sticking out halfway across the hearthrug. On him
it looked graceful, but Hester didn't feel graceful, not
with her straight skirt riding up above her knees and
with her rather scuffed slippers on prominent display.
She was also at a disadvantage, almost half lying in the
chair as she was. Her mother was looking down on
her, making her feel like a child or a naughty
housemaid who had been caught larking about. She
straightened herself, pulling a couple of cushions
beneath her to raise herself a bit.

'Why are you here?' she asked baldly. 'And don't try
to tell me you're interested in how I'm getting on,
because I shan't believe you.'

'No, I don't suppose you would.' Vilma stubbed out
her half finished cigarette and lit another immediately.
'As a matter of fact, I came to ask whether you had
any spare money.'

'About five pounds in my purse and nearly two
hundred in the bank,' Hester said flatly as she poured
herself another cup of tea.

'Oh lord, another one!' Vilma lifted her eyes to the
ceiling in a kind of mute appeal to fate. 'You're the
same as me—married to one of these damn Greeks
who provides us with everything we need. Who
houses, feeds and clothes us, gives us everything we
want except hard cash.' She drew on the cigarette and
let the smoke trickle down her nostrils. 'I'm sorry
about that, truly I am, but if you can't help me, I shall
have to take the other alternative.'

'Oh, get on with it!' Hester descended to crudeness. 'Say what you have to say and cut the cackle. Just at the moment you're not making much sense.'

'You're so like your father, my dear!' Vilma shook her head and shrugged. 'He always had to have everything laid on the line for him—one could hint and hint, he never understood until everything was put to him in words of one syllable. To be blunt, I need a rather large sum of money and I need it quickly. I had two options—you because I thought you couldn't have spent what you had from me and the other—well, I'd rather not mention that yet, not until you've had a rethink.'

'No need for a rethink.' Hester gave a tight smile. 'The money I had from you—I had a use for it, and the day after I received it I put it to that use. I don't have a penny of it left.'

'Pity,' Vilma made a little moue of almost regret. 'You leave me no alternative.'

'Will you get on with it!' Hester seethed with exasperation as she looked at her watch and checked it against the carriage clock on the mantlepiece. 'It's nearly twenty past three and I have to leave here at four-fifteen to pick Katy up from school. I've no time to waste on hints and innuendoes.'

Vilma shrugged. 'I'm a gambler, my dear, I like to play the tables and usually I win, but last year was a bad year. I lost far more than I could afford. Of course, I couldn't include gambling losses when I made a list of my debts for your husband, I tried that once before and he refused to pay, so when, because of you, he cut my allowance almost to nothing, I started getting unpleasant letters from the place where I play. Lately, the letters have become more than unpleasant, they're almost threatening, so I have to find money and find it fast. I've tried gambling on credit, but it's always the same when you do that—you lose!'

'And I can't help you.' Hester felt dismay and a faint pity. 'What's this alternative?'

'Simply that I play Athene's game for her.' Vilma took a sip at her cup, found the tea had cooled so that it was undrinkable and put the cup down. 'She wants you out, my dear,' she continued, 'and I suppose one can't blame her. She wants Demetrios and she wants her daughter, and you're in the way, so you'll have to go, and if you won't go willingly, she's cooked up a little scheme.'

'Athene wants her daughter?' Hester looked her astonishment. It was an assumed astonishment, but she thought she did it very well.

'Katy! Don't say you haven't noticed the resemblance.' Vilma smiled wryly. 'Even I did that, and I'm not noted for noticing much. They're as alike as two peas from the same pod. It was a long time ago,' she added, 'and Athene was being pushed into one of those marriages Greek fathers are so fond of arranging, and in any case, they'd never have let her marry Demetrios—but she's a widow now and a wealthy one. She wants her man back, and her daughter.'

'Then she'd better speak about it to Demetrios,' Hester said flatly. 'I'm not equipped to make a decision like that, and in any case, maybe he isn't all that keen any longer. As you said, it was all a long time ago, and tastes change.'

'Then you don't know?' Vilma registered surprise. 'They went off to Athens together, you know, and he didn't stay in the hotel as he usually does. This time he lived with Athene at her villa. When he went on to Crete and Cyprus, she came back to London and told me all about it.'

'Why didn't she come and tell me?' Hester had gone cold. It was one thing to love a man when you didn't know about his other women, but knowing about them made all the difference. She felt physically sick, she wanted to rush away somewhere quiet and on her own where she could burst into a storm of weeping. She'd been the most complete fool, she must have given herself away a thousand times. . . . Vilma broke in on her thoughts and she had to pay attention to what her mother was saying or Vilma would have something to crow about.

'You don't know Athene very well, do you? She can't bear to be in the limelight, she prefers to be offstage, directing things. No,' Vilma lit another cigarette, the third in less than an hour, 'when all this is over, Athene wants to come out of it with not a stain on her reputation.'

'She wants a hell of a lot,' Hester growled, conscious of a rising anger. 'And how does she expect it to happen all at once? You know the divorce laws as well as I do, if not better. Haven't you told her nobody can do anything for three years?'

'I did make the point,' Vilma admitted, 'but Athene says she'll manage very well as long as you clear out, and if you won't go willingly, she'll make you—she has it all worked out. That woman has a mind like a computer.'

'How?' Hester forced the word from her lips with a studied nonchalance.

'So simple,' Vilma laughed; it sounded a bit forced, and now her face was showing strain, she looked every day of her age. 'Yesterday afternoon, at about three o'clock, you phoned me. No, don't try to say you weren't even here, that you were taking tea in the vicarage or something equally bucolic. I phoned *you*, don't you remember? And when you answered, I hung up without speaking. . . .'

'I thought it was a wrong number,' Hester frowned. 'Do tell me what I was supposed to have said. As an interested party, I think I ought to know.'

'You asked for more money, of course. As I said, Demetrios was giving you everything but plain cash, and you married him for that, not for a house or a car or anything you couldn't convert to money. Of course, this time I was lucky, somebody was with me and I sent her to listen in on the extension. Rather a crafty move, don't you think? It gave me what I didn't have before when you tried your first bit of blackmail. I now have a witness.'

'Athene!' Hester nodded. 'A very nice try—and are you going to tell my husband if I play it awkward?'

'Of course.' Vilma's laugh was rather forced. 'I shan't have to if you're sensible and leave him. If you walk out tomorrow. . . .'

'I can't do that,' Hester protested. 'There's Katy, I can't leave her at the drop of a hat.'

'You'd better,' Vilma said grimly, 'because if you don't, I shall have to tell Demetrios what you've been up to and he'll throw you out. But it needn't be as nasty as that, not if you use your head. I don't want to do this, but as I've explained, I don't have much option. Athene's going to give me the money I need when you go, so save yourself a lot of trouble and go quietly. He'll probably be quite generous and you needn't go empty-handed.'

'You and Athene, you're a couple of—oh, I can't think of a word bad enough for you!'

'Save your breath,' Vilma advised. 'You can slate Athene all you want but be sensible when it comes to me. I talked her into giving you this chance. Without that, you'd have been a dead duck, and really I've little choice. You're younger than I am and able to earn your own living, whereas me, I'm dependent on Sandros, and if he hears about my little failing, *he'll* throw me out, and what would I do at my age? It would be the finish of me.' She rose from the chair and walked elegantly to the door, where she paused and turned back.

'You *are* like your father,' she said. 'You've got a lot of his honesty and you're just as damn naïve as he was. He thought we should marry, he had some dream about a rose-covered cottage and love everlasting, but I never went for that "better a dinner of herbs where love is" thing. I'll put up with the hatred as long as the ox is well cooked and served with mushrooms and a wine sauce on a silver dish. And don't start thinking Demetrios will disbelieve Athene—remember, he's just spent four days with her in Athens, reliving the love of his life. She told me he was happier than he'd been for years.'

Hester sat rigid in the chair, listening to the closing door, the tap of high heels on the polished tiles of the hall and the gentle thud of the front door. Then there was the sound of the Lancia starting up and the crunch of the wheels on the gravel of the drive. After that, only silence.

She felt old and beaten, older even than her mother, and she wanted to run screaming from the house to lose herself somewhere and die, but that was impossible. There was Katy to be collected from school and then the party.

With a groan, she pulled herself out of the chair and made her way upstairs. She still felt sick and her head was beginning to ache, pain stabbing through her temples. There was another hard knot of pain in her chest, hurting her when she breathed and bringing tears to her eyes, but they wouldn't fall, they stayed there, smarting beneath her eyelids.

Somehow she drove herself towards the bathroom, almost feeling her way upstairs, and remembering what Demetrios had called her practical approach, she took her own advice and swallowed a couple of aspirins with a drink of water from a tooth mug, then splashed cold water all over her face.

Gradually the pain receded and anger began to take the place of misery. One bad thing she had done, and that was for a good cause, but him—if she'd been physically capable of strangling him, she'd have done it. He was nothing but a cheat—she hated him—as soon as she saw him tonight, she'd tell him exactly what she thought of him and walk out, *and* she wouldn't need to be paid for doing it. He could take his magnanimity and strangle on it! She didn't want a penny, she wouldn't touch a coin or note of his filthy money.

But she'd wait for all this until the party was over and Katy was in bed and asleep. Poor little Katy, what chance would she have with parents such as this, a scheming woman and an adulterer? She shivered again and felt the headache growing to unbearable proportions.

Better to go and fetch Katy now so that they would be back in the house when Demetrios arrived. Looking in the bathroom mirror, Hester swore, every bad word she could think of, intoned like a litany of hate, and when she had exhausted her vocabulary, she went downstairs and out into the fresh air, got into the Mini and drove steadily to the school.

'You're late, I thought you were never coming, has Papa arrived yet? Did he make you late?' Katy was dancing with impatience at the school gates.

'No to both of your questions.' By this time, Hester was in command of herself. Swiftly she manufactured an excuse. 'Some bother with the barbecue—I had to fetch fresh charcoal from Esher. Sorry about it, but I wanted it to be perfect. Little things like that would have spoilt your party, we'd have had to cook your burgers under the electric grill in the kitchen.'

Katy nodded understandingly. 'And you're sad because Papa hasn't come home yet. I expect he can't help it, the plane might have been delayed—it often happens.' She spoke with all the experience of a well seasoned traveller and Hester could have kissed her for being so blessedly normal.

'Everything's ready for you, darling.' Her lips twisted in a mockery of a smile, but Katy was so happy, so excited she surely wouldn't notice. 'What frock are you planning on wearing?'

'No frocks,' Katy said firmly. 'We've talked it over, me and the other girls, and we're going to wear jeans and tops so we won't be cold when the sun goes down and one of them—the girls, you know—is going to bring some extra records for the hi-fi. It's going to be a wonderful party! Thank you so much, Hes, for arranging it for me and for the burgers and barbecue and everything.'

At home, Katy's first call was on her puppy and she came back to the kitchen, carrying him and puffing under the weight.

'I think Papa's going to be surprised when he comes and sees him, don't you, Hes? He's grown an awful lot in two weeks.'

'So have his puddles,' Hester answered darkly. 'And that reminds me, he's left one in the conservatory, you'd better clear it up before your guests arrive. You don't want them sloshing through one of his miniature lakes! Filthy beast, aren't you?' She fondled the pup's ears and Katy went off happily, carrying a sponge mop and a bucket of clean water, with the culprit following her closely.

When they had gone, Hester set about her final preparations, arranging the tables on the patio and taking out the boxes of food, but even being busy couldn't stop her thinking, and she wished she had Mia with her. At least she could have shared her troubles. She had asked Mia down for the weekend, but her foster-sister had refused point blank.

'It's not as if you were on your own, Hes,' Mia's voice had come cool and clear over the phone. 'You've got the little girl with you and she's bound to tell her father.'

'So what?' At that time, Hester had been beligerent.

'So, you'll have to explain who I am, and then that'll lead to more explanations. You'll end up telling him about Flo and how you spent the money you had from him. He'll think we're sponging off you as soon as his back's turned. No, love, I won't come unless he's there and invites me himself!' And that had been that. Mia might not be a blazing, vital personality, but she was as obstinate as all get out when she had an idea firmly in her mind. So there was nothing to do but sweat it out herself—on her own, meanwhile giving the appearance of bright normality for the sake of Katy and the other girls.

She succeeded better than her wildest dreams. Nobody suspected a thing, not even Katy, when at half past nine, Demetrios had still not arrived. She was disappointed, it showed in her huge dark eyes, but she was also phlegmatic. These things happened. Katy was proud of her father and she had wanted to show him off to her friends, but it was not to be, and there was always another time.

CHAPTER NINE

By half past ten, the house seemed quiet after the uproar of the last three hours. All Katy's guests were gone, ferried home by obliging parents who perfectly understood that Hester couldn't manage seven little girls by herself, and Katy had gone off to bed, tired but happy. Hester employed herself in getting the house straight, and although it was probably bad for him, Katy's pup dined off bits of beefburger, abandoned pieces of buttered rolls and all the crisps and peanuts that remained uneaten. As a second course, he polished off a large amount of melting icecream and she put him to sleep in his packing case bed, grinning as he hiccuped. He was much more fun than a waste disposal unit!

Demetrios called at half past eleven, brief and matter-of-fact. His plane had been delayed by engine trouble and had landed at Athens with more of the same trouble, then the passengers had been fed, a few at a time, into other planes bound for London. As the tourist season was getting into full swing, most of the planes could take no more than two or three people, so he had had a long wait before he was once again airborne. He was tired and didn't think it wise to drive down straight away, so he'd wait till morning—this was a call from a public phone at the airport, there were a number of people waiting to use it after him, so he would tell Hester all about it tomorrow—and with a 'Goodnight, darling', he had hung up.

Hester stared at the circle of perforated black plastic

and nodded grimly, 'So that's your line, is it?' she enquired of the mouthpiece before she slammed the receiver back into the cradle, then she smiled grimly at herself and her own naïvety. Had she expected any other sort of telephone call? Of course she hadn't! She was making a big drama out of nothing. The best thing she could do was to go straight to bed, get a good night's sleep and wake refreshed and able to cope.

The 'good night's sleep' was a washout. She lay staring into the darkness while her mind went round and round, getting nowhere. One part of her mind accepted Vilma's story, but a calm, sensible part of her dismissed it. Vilma was merely retailing a story which had been told to her and she probably believed it was the truth—there had been the vaguest hint of pity in her baby blue eyes.

By the time the grey light of the false dawn had pushed some of the night shadows away, Hester had arrived at an inescapable conclusion. Vilma had told her the truth. Athene was a beautiful woman with a smouldering passion beneath her calm surface—if she offered, it would take a saint to refuse her, and Demetrios was no saint. He and Athene had been lovers in the past and they'd probably be lovers again and Katy was the tie between them, a constant reminder of how it had been once and how it could be again.

And Demetrios wouldn't feel in the least guilty about it. If she, Hester, asked him, he would admit it without any shame, and in any case—she punched the pillows and closed her eyes firmly—she was going, and not because of Vilma's silly threat, which didn't frighten her a bit. She was going because it was the right thing to do. Demetrios, Athene and Katy belonged together, they were a family, whereas all she was was a bystander, somebody who had been drawn in by accident of circumstances.

She would have a little sleep until half past seven, then she would do all the usual things and take Katy to school. When she came back, she would pack her clothes, wait for Demetrios, explain that she had to go and that would be that. She wouldn't be emotional about it either!

The morning light was cruel to her as she looked in the bathroom mirror after her shower. Her eyelids were puffy and there were violet stains beneath her eyes to tell of a sleeplesss night, but that sort of thing could be hidden and she went off to the bedroom and after dressing, set about concealing the evidence with a tinted foundation and a load of eye-shadow. She couldn't take the look of strain out of her eyes, but she could disguise it and did, so that Katy's sharp eyes didn't notice anything unusual when they sat down to breakfast.

'Your papa phoned last night, he'd arrived in London but he was too tired to drive down. He'll be here this morning.' Hester poured tea and strove for a calm approach.

Katy nodded while she spooned up cereal. 'He doesn't like driving when he's tired, he says that's when people have accidents,' she observed, looking up from her plate, and Hester caught her breath. For just a second, all resemblance to Athene was wiped from Katy's face and in it's place Demetrios looked out of her eyes and her mouth curved into his smile, thoroughly adult and understanding. 'Papa says we need never worry about him, he doesn't take chances.'

'I'll be taking a few, trying to get you to school on time, if you don't rush your breakfast a bit!' Hester rose from the table and as she passed behind Katy, she squeezed her shoulder with a fond hand. 'You're happy, dear? This is what you want?'

'Of course.' Katy pushed aside her cereal bowl and helped herself to toast. 'It's what I've wanted for a long time, ever since Miss Mungo gave me books about girls. A proper home, not living in hotels, and a papa who came home every evening so I could tell him what I'd been doing all day and have him help me with my homework,' specially the maths—I'm no good at that.' She sighed. 'I'm afraid I'm going to come bottom of the class, I don't understand algebra one little bit.'

'But you'll be top in French,' Hester comforted. 'You can't have it all ways.'

Driving back from delivering Katy to school, Hester rehearsed what she was going to say to Demetrios when he arrived. She had decided against slipping away unnoticed—that smacked of cowardice. She strung the words out aloud, trying them to see if they sounded right and gave the correct impression of dignity.

'Had you come home last night. . . .' No, that wasn't any good—start again.

'While you've been away, I've been thinking'—that was much better—'and I've come to the conclusion that this bargain we made isn't going to work.' So far, so good—she wouldn't mention anything about Vilma's visit, that ground was too treacherous and she might find herself bogged down in emotional phrases like, 'I can't live with a man when I know he has a mistress whom he prefers to me'. Things like that were out! It had to be kept calm and practical.

She kept on mulling over what she would say, changing a word here and there while she swiftly packed her suitcases in readiness for her departure, and when everything was ready, she went across to the dressing table mirror and tried it out again—she had to be word-perfect.

'While you've been away, I've been thinking, and I've come to the conclusion that this strange bargain we made isn't going to work. You don't really need a wife; a housekeeper, a nice one, would do just as well, so I've decided to leave you and go back to London. Please don't bother to see me out, I'm going to phone for a taxi, and there are loads of trains. . . .'

'. . . .Then I shall require an immediate repayment of twenty thousand pounds.' Demetrios' voice came from the bedroom door which she couldn't see in the mirror. 'Do you have the cash handy?'

'You know I haven't!' She swung round to face him and all her fine, calm, practical words died on her lips, to be replaced by hot, angry ones—the ones which she'd decided not to use. 'And I wouldn't give it to you if I had. A bargain's a bargain, but you've cheated on me, so that washes it all out. I'm free to go.'

'Not until you've paid your debt and explained why, when you should be greeting me with affection, making up to me for being without you for two weeks—you're behaving,' he stopped and looked at her—'and looking like a harpy. Did you know your hair's come down?'

With a quick gasp of dismay, Hester turned back to the mirror, and nearly wept at what she saw. During her rehearsal, she had been concentrating on her expression, trying out a haughty curl to her lip and a sophisticated droop of her eyelids—now she looked at the total picture and groaned. She was unbecomingly flushed and several tumbled strands of hair were falling across her shoulders. Hastily and with trembling fingers, she pushed them back into the loose coil at the back of her neck, and while she was doing it, Demetrios crossed to the bed to lift the lid of one of the cases and examine the contents.

'So,' he murmured with an aggravating smile about his mouth, 'you were practising your farewell speech, but haven't you made a small mistake? No nice housekeeper would perform *all* your duties—she'd walk out if I expected her to go to bed with me and she mightn't be the right age for childbearing. What's going on?' He made the enquiry mildly. 'Or have I come back to a madhouse?'

'You could call it that.' Hester looked at her husband and then looked hastily away again. It wouldn't do to indulge in sentimental thoughts about how two weeks in the Mediterranean sunshine had darkened his skin to a warm, deep olive tint—how the open neck of his white shirt flattered the strong column of his throat—how good he looked, like a glass of water to a thirsty traveller or food to a starving woman—She pulled herself together.

'Yes,' she went on, fighting against a shortage of breath which threatened to make her voice wobble, 'you could very well call it a madhouse. The whole set-up's screwy and the deeper in I get, the screwier it becomes. That's why I'm getting out, while I still have my sanity. Oh!' she squealed with temper as, with a wide swing of his arm, Demetrios swept the cases from the bed. They tumbled to the floor and one sprang open, scattering clothing onto the carpet. 'Now look what you've done!' she scolded. 'I'll have to pack that lot all over again!'

'You'll do nothing of the kind.' Demetrios advanced on her until his broad shoulders filled her vision completely. Her heart gave one tremendous thump and started to beat erratically and her mouth went dry from fright. 'Nobody's going anywhere any more today, and certainly not you.' He made it very definite.

'You can't stop me!' Hester flared, pushing past him bravely and starting to gather up the tumbled garments, ramming them back in the case higgledy-piggledy and forcing the lid down on the jumbled contents. 'You forgot Katy's birthday, you didn't even send her a card'—she made it sound like one of the seven deadly sins, 'and like I said, you've been cheating on me. That wipes the slate clean. . . . Oooh! Don't stand there looking like a pillar of virtue,' she raged. 'I know all about it, I know what you've been up to, and if you think you can hop out of my bed and into Athene's whenever you fancy, you've got another think coming! She might have the stomach for that sort of thing, but I won't tolerate it. You—you lecher! I will *not* be made a convenience of!'

'What makes you think I've been going to bed with Athene?'

Hester scrambled to her feet and aimed a kick at his shins. It was rather spoiled by the fact that she was wearing soft shoes so it didn't have quite the effect she desired, but the doing of it relieved her feelings.

'I don't just think, I *know*!' she squealed with wrath. 'You and she went to Athens together and you didn't stay at the hotel as you said you were going to—you didn't tell me that, but I know. You shacked up with her at her villa or whatever you call it. . . .' The rest of what she'd been going to say died on her lips as Demetrios advanced on her and she cringed when his hands came hard on her shoulders.

'Frightened, Hester?' Demetrios spoke between his

teeth. 'You've every right to be. I was *not* sleeping with Athene. I've never slept with her.'

'Liar!' she spat at him, raising her voice unconsciously.

'Be quiet!' he commanded, giving her a shake. 'Do you want the woman to hear us quarrelling?'

'Who cares!' She tried to squirm away from his hands, but it was no use, he was holding her shoulders as though he never meant to let go. 'She can't anyway, she's not here today, she's taking one of the children to the dentist. And don't try to change the subject—I'm talking about Katy, she's a living proof that you're lying. I know you said she's your adopted daughter, but she's more than that, isn't she? She's yours and she's Athene's as well. That's something nobody could hide—why, even Vilma spotted the likeness, and she was only looking at the photograph in the sitting-room. . . .' With a little cry of dismay, Hester covered her mouth with shaking fingers. Damn her unruly tongue! That was the worst of losing her temper, all sorts of things came spilling out, and among them the one thing she hadn't wanted him to know. And then she realised he'd missed it, it had gone right over his head.

'You bloody little idiot!' His fingers bit deeper into her shoulders, bruising the delicate bones, but she welcomed the pain—it kept her fighting mad.

'Don't you dare swear at me!'

'Swear at you? I'll damn well strangle you, and who could blame me? It's a wonder I haven't beaten you! *Will you listen*, instead of tearing into me like a wildcat! I *told* you, Athene and I are distant cousins—to be exact, our grandmothers were sisters—identical twin sisters. Yes,' as she started to wriggle again to be free of him, 'I know Katy looks like Athene, but that likeness doesn't prove she's Athene's daughter, it merely proves she's mine! Will you get that through your stupid little head? *Mine*, not Athene's!' and then, emphasising every word with a shake, '*Do-you-believe-me-now?*'

Hester collapsed like a pricked balloon, all her fight gone and with only bewilderment and an aching regret left.

'Yes,' she stood quite still under his hands. 'Yes, I'll believe you—you've never lied to me—Oh hell!—You won't understand this, but I'm going!'

'Over my dead body!' Demetrios let go of her shoulders and swept her up in his arms, striding with her to the bed. 'You've just said we're alone in the house, which makes this a very good opportunity to have things straightened out. We're going to have a talk, we'll love each other a little, and then we'll have some lunch.' He put her down gently on the bed and dropped his long length beside her, drawing her close, and with a hand on the back of her head, he pushed her face into the curve of his neck.

'No, don't wriggle, Hester. I've got something to tell you, and it'll be easier if I can't see your face.'

'Why?' she muttered, feeling the skin of his throat beneath her lips. 'It'll make an awful mess of your shirt.'

'Because it's a sad little story and I'm not proud of the part I played in it.' He rested his chin on the top of her head. 'And my shirt doesn't matter. So be quiet and don't interrupt, I just want you to listen.'

'All ears,' she assured him, feeling suddenly gay as though she'd come home to warmth, tenderness and love. 'Waggling ears,' she added, choking back a sob which was half laughter.

'And it's no time for jokes,' Demetrios chided her

seriously. 'I said it's rather a sad little story, nearly fourteen years old. At that time, my father had sent me to Cyprus where we were opening our first hotel; I had to learn the business from the ground up. I went out in April, a young man, not yet twenty-one and, like all young men, very full of myself; brash, greedy and a bit careless. One of the receptionists was a girl, about eighteen, and we became friendly. She was an orphan, her father had been a Greek Cypriot and her mother an Armenian from Thrace—that served as a common bond, as my mother was also from Thrace.'

'But I thought your mother was Turkish.' Hester hadn't wanted to interrupt, but she wanted to get things straight.

'She was,' he chuckled as she raised her head from his shoulder. 'You don't know very much about Greece or the Greeks, do you? Both Albania and Turkey have Greek minorities and there are Turks, Slavs and Armenians living in Greece, mostly in Thrace. There are also Vlachs, who speak a Latin-based language, and some people known as Pomaks who are Bulgarian Moslems—but, to get back to this girl, she had only one relative left, an old woman who lived up in the mountains near Mount Olympus; she was lonely, starved of affection and with nobody to spend her own affection on. She chose me, we became more than friendly and, as I said, I was greedy and careless. I took what she offered without a second thought.' Demetrios paused and when he started speaking again, his voice was deep with regret.

'In the September, I was sent for to come back to England—my parents had been in a traffic accident; my father was killed outright and my mother, although terribly injured, was still alive. Naturally I came back at once, after promising the girl I'd return as soon as possible, but I couldn't. My mother needed me and I stayed with her until she died, which was about six months later. I wrote to the girl, she wrote back to me, a pleasant letter saying she was well and waiting for my return, but I never answered that letter. I made excuses to myself—I was busy; with my father dead, there was a lot to do, a lot to learn—I couldn't leave my mother—any excuse but the real one, which was that I didn't love the girl, that she was like a holiday romance, she had no part in my real world.'

Hester raised her head and looked into his eyes. She thought she knew the rest of the story, and the pain reflected in his face told her she was at least partly right. 'But you did go back eventually?

'Mmm,' he pushed her head down again. 'But too late. The girl had left the hotel some time before I returned, there was a rumour among the staff that she was pregnant and, knowing her—she wasn't a promiscuous girl or anything like that—I knew the child was mine, so I set out to find her. There was only one place she could have gone, back to the old woman, so I went there. The village was bad enough, Hester—you've no idea of the poverty, but where the old woman lived, farther up the mountain, it was indescribable. She had a bit of land. Pasturage for a few goats which were her livelihood and a tiny house, one room downstairs and a bit of a loft. There were no facilities, every drop of water had to be carried from a spring, and that was where the girl had gone and where my daughter was born.' His voice dropped to almost a whisper, thick, hoarse and full of pain. 'She wasn't a strong girl and she'd had a hard time, out in all weathers with the goats—there was very little money and no doctor—nobody to fetch him if one had been available—only the old woman to do everything, and she was very angry when I arrived. I don't think she would have minded so much if the baby had died as long as the girl lived—as she said, the girl was of some use even if it was only to milk the goats—but the baby was an added burden and she was too old for it.'

'But the girl was dead,' Hester muttered into his chest. 'What did you do then?'

'Gave the old crone enough money to keep her in splendour for the rest of her life, and even then she wasn't satisfied until I hired a boy from the village to care for her damn goats—and I brought the baby back to Limassol with me. She was only a few weeks old, but her resemblance to my grandmother was marked, even then, and I called her Khadija, after my own mother. It wasn't until I imported Miss Mungo three years ago that we called her Katy. Miss Mungo couldn't get her tongue round "Khadija", so she called her after the initials on the cases. Khadija Thalassis—K. T.—Katy—it stuck, and Katy seemed to like it. She wanted a home in England with me and an English name to go with it.'

He lifted Hester's head with a finger under her chin. 'Do you think very badly of me? I've tried to mend my ways. Since then, there have been other women, but I made sure they weren't innocents. They knew what they were doing, they knew the rules of the game.'

'And Athene?' Hester looked into his eyes, searching for something.

'Not Athene,' he said definitely. 'She had a marriage all arranged for her, a rich, suitable one with a man old enough to be her father. She had to go to his bed unspoiled, so our little flirtation was just that and no more. Afterwards, she told me, things could be different, but by that time I'd learned a bit more, and besides, I liked her husband, so I tactfully went away.'

The room seemed to Hester to be warmer and the sunlight brighter. Daringly, she dropped a kiss on his mouth which was shaped to receive it. 'Very noble of you,' she murmured. 'The sort of action which shows great will power and a pure mind, and,' she sobered and her face became grave. 'I *do* understand about Katy's mother. That sort of thing alters a person— without it, you wouldn't be what you are now.' Humour bubbled up irrepressibly in her so that she chuckled. 'Not exactly a saint, but liveable with. Oh lord!' Her expression was comical. 'What you must have thought of me that first time when you forced your way into my bedsit!'

'You want to know?' Demetrios's eyes gleamed beneath half closed lids. 'I wasn't liking you when I arrived, I'd set out with some preconceived ideas based on my own experiences. Katy's mother wasn't to blame for having—er—fallen by the wayside, that was all my fault, so I was biassed in favour of Vilma, although I never did like her very much. That's something I can't explain either. It was a gut reaction, because she's been a good wife to my uncle, she hasn't caused a breath of scandal. I thought you were being unpleasant to the wrong parent—see what I mean?'

'Not your fault.' Hester shook her head, trying to be just. 'I didn't make a very good impression—I must have sounded like one of the Furies!'

'You certainly were't very accommodating.' He shifted her to a more comfortable position in his arms. 'Twenty thousand in used notes in a paper bag—you sounded like a gangster's moll, but,' his lips curved in a reminiscent smile, 'you were so beautiful, and after you'd slapped me down, I started to make excuses for you, and by the time you practically threw me out, I'd made up my mind Vilma should give you the money and I was plotting how to get you into bed. I was sorry about that later, but at the time, I thought you knew the ropes. I'd some idea of hiding you away in a love nest nobody knew about, keeping you to myself, but something in your manner when we were in the restaurant made me realise that, after all, you weren't the type, you wouldn't go along with anything like that, so I grabbed at a couple of fortuitous circumstances and asked you to marry me.'

'Asked!' Hester squeaked with indignation. 'You didn't ask! It was an "either or" thing, an ultimatum. You forced me. . . .'

'And after I kissed you, I knew why.' Demetrios found her mouth and there was a long silence. 'Mmm,' he raised his head. 'It's a bit different now—that first time, you were a bit passionate, but underneath there was a shy, beguiling innocence that took my breath away. You were taking the first step with me and I wanted to make sure you took every other step as well, and with me, nobody else! I was in love with you, Hester. I still am, and I think I always will be. I wanted you and I knew I could make you want me— rather basic, I'm afraid, but I thought we could go on from there to bigger and better things.'

Hester closed her eyes to hide the wild, leaping happiness in them as she pulled his head down to hers. 'Oh, my love,' she whispered, 'my very, very dear, dear love. Isn't it wonderful?'

'And equally wonderful that we're alone in the house,' he teased. 'Otherwise the daily would have been pushing her vacuum round by now and we'd have had to move!'

'Wake up, you disgusting little slut!' Demetrios was standing at the side of the bed with a cup of coffee in his hand. 'You've no thought for your family at all, lying here in bed till noon. What are we supposed to be having for lunch? All I can find in the fridge is a box of chipped steaks.'

Hester half opened her lids and looked at him drowsily. 'Spares,' she stifled a yawn. 'In case we ran out of beefburgers for Katy's birthday party.'

'Strange food for a birthday party.' Demetrios' eyebrows rose.

'My dear man, my very dear man!' Hester struggled to sit up in bed, pulling the sheet up to cover herself and flushing when she saw the derisory glint in his eyes. 'Where have you been this last ten years? Jelly and blancmange are O.K. for children, young ladies demand something a little more sophisticated like a barbecue on the patio and a jam session in the lounge after they've stuffed themselves. I bought beefburgers because I didn't think we could barbecue steaks properly. Oh dear!' as she looked around the bedroom. 'This place is one hell of a mess, there are clothes scattered everywhere. Do you always leave your trousers hung up on the floor, or is it a habit you've picked up over the last fortnight?'

He sat down on the side of the bed and ran a long finger over her bare shoulder. 'Do we have everything ironed out now, my darling?'

'Nearly everything.' She took a sip of the coffee. 'That's good, better than when I make it,' she told him.

'Are you hinting?' His eyes narrowed with laughter. 'Because let me tell you, my darling witch, I've no intention of taking over the commissariat duties, not when I'm keeping a woman in the house.'

'And you, taught the hotel trade from the bottom up,' she marvelled. 'Didn't you have to start in the kitchens?'

'I did, washing up!' Demetrios became insistent. 'Are you satisfied with your share of our bargain, that's what I'm trying to find out.'

'Hooh!' She handed back the empty coffee cup. 'You're just looking for compliments. You want me to say something to bolster your ego, but how can I? I've no standard of comparison. . . .'

'And you never will have.' He stopped trailing his fingers across her shoulder to tighten his hand on her upper arm. 'And that's a threat, not a promise. Now,' he aimed a slap at her hip, 'get up and you shall have your lunch cooked for you just this once as a reward for being a loving wife.'

When he had gone, Hester scrambled herself into the bathroom and stood under the shower for a few minutes. All the clouds had gone except one, and that one loomed big and black in her sky. She hadn't feared Vilma's threat, not when she had been ready to pack and leave as soon as Demetrios came home, but now, everything was different.

She wondered how Demetrios would take such a story, and to give credit to Athene, it was a very good story. There was nothing unbelievable about it. What she had done once, she could easily be believed to have done again, especially when she still hadn't told him why she had done it in the first place.

While she rubbed herself dry and struggled into clean underwear, Hester pondered the problem. She could tell him now, tell him about Flo and the clinic—the reason she'd wanted the money, but—her mouth firmed. No, she wouldn't. What would his love be worth if it had to be founded on reason?

And then she smiled wryly at herself. What had hers been worth either? She'd been all too ready to condemn, although, even in condemnation, she'd still loved him and, even if he had been with Athene, she would have allowed him to wheedle himself back into her arms—but no, she couldn't tell, not yet, not even to save her happiness, not if Vilma's tale killed his love stone dead.

It was strange how his thoughts seemed to follow hers—when she entered the kitchen, sniffed and gazed appreciatively at the well laid table, the bowl of green salad—when Demetrios had seated her and spread her napkin with a flourish that made her giggle and then placed the dish of fried, chipped steaks on the table——

'You never did explain what you wanted all that money for, or even what you did with it.'

'No, I didn't, did I?' she agreed amiably. "And I'm not going to, not yet. Are you consumed with curiosity?'

He chuckled. 'Not a bit. I'd like to know, of course, and you'll tell me some time. Answer me one question, though—did you give it to your hairdressing friend? Because if you did and it was an investment, from what I hear, your prospects are pretty sound, that young man's going places. America, I hope. I prefer to have an ocean between him and you.'

'Silly!' Hester reproved without saying 'yes' or 'no'. 'Crispin's certainly going places, and I also hope it's America—Hollywood preferably, because it's where he's always wanted to go. He aims to be a second Vidal Sassoon, and he's good enough, but we were only ever friends. He hasn't much time for girls, his career is far too important to him. Truly, he was never anything more than a very good employer and a friend when it didn't interfere with his career. If you ever threw me out, he'd take me back at once, not because he has any feelings for me but because I'm a good hairdresser, that's all.'

'It had better be,' Demetrios observed darkly.

Hester kept everything very light and merry for the next two days. She was waiting for the blow to fall, but before it fell, there was love and laughter, passion and sweet fulfilment, so she made the most of it. It might be snatched away from her at any moment, and she was determined to have as many memories as possible to carry with her into the lean, dark years ahead.

CHAPTER TEN

THE telephone rang insistently, and Hester let it ring while she looked round the sunlit kitchen, planning where she would start—not that it took much planning. There was the dishwasher to load with the breakfast things and there was a small pile of good china and some crystal glasses left over from dinner last night—those wouldn't go in the machine, they would have to be done by hand—and the daily woman had once again rung to say she wouldn't be coming this morning. Hester sighed and hoped that if and when she had a family, her children would be a little more healthy than the daily's, who all seemed to be in daily need of dentristy, injections or a visit from the doctor.

The telephone kept up its brr—brrr hopefully as though it knew that if it did it long enough, somebody would dive to take the phone off the hook, and at last, with a sigh and a reluctant step, Hester went into the hall to answer it. Demetrios, who had given himself a few days off to get over his Mediterranean trip, had been callous about the non-appearance of the daily, but had relieved her of the task of driving Katy to school, and he was being very sluggish about getting back.

Vilma's light, chill voice came over the wire. 'You're still there, Hester. Do you think that's wise?'

Hester glared at the mouthpiece. She had been expecting this—possibly why she hadn't wanted to answer the phone for the last two days—and she yet had to decide what to say or do. She'd have to play it by ear.

'Surely neither you nor Athene expected me to vanish in a puff of smoke?' she answered irritably. 'I can't abandon Katy without making some provision for her.'

An arm came round her waist and a hand took the receiver from her fingers and she turned to find Demetrios at her elbow.

'Creeping up on me again!' she snarled softly.

'Having trouble with the boy-friend?' he countered in a low murmur. 'What's this about making provision for Katy? I'll have a word with him myself, make it quite plain you haven't a moment to spare,' and he clapped the receiver to his ear.

Hester hitched herself up on her toes to get as close to the earpiece as possible. She wanted to hear what was said, and she grinned sarcastically as his brief 'Hello' was met with Vilma's, 'Is that you, Demos? I thought you'd be in town at your office.'

Putting her tongue out at him, Hester dropped back on to her heels and with a flounce went back to the kitchen, where she banged pots and pans about on the stainless steel draining board and sang tunelessly at the top of her voice, before Demetrios came back into the kitchen and put a hand over her mouth.

'You shouldn't do that,' he reproved. 'You've got a lot of volume, but you're tone-deaf. Vilma seems to be in a bit of a knot, something she doesn't want Sandros to know about, so we're meeting her in town this afternoon. I've phoned the school and asked them to keep Katy with the boarders for the night—that'll save us rushing back.'

'Little Lord Put-it-right,' Hester scowled down into

the perfectly clean sink. 'I don't see why I have to go with you, and I don't care for Katy being fobbed off with the boarders when she has a perfectly good home.'

'She'll be boarding next year in any case,' Demetrios told her calmly.

'Boarding?' Hester's voice rose an octave. 'For heaven's sake, why? We only live five miles from the school, and it's no trouble to drive her there and bring her home. . . .'

'But next year, you might be otherwise occupied.' His calm broke up and his eyes sparkled. 'You can't drive a Mini while you're dandling a baby on your lap.'

'I don't want Katy to board,' Hester said mutinously. 'I don't think she'll be happy. . . .'

'Nonsense,' he broke in on her. 'She'll be perfectly happy once she settles in, she's quite well able to look after herself and very adaptable. It'll be good for her, and besides. . . .'

'Oh yes, I know,' she was becoming cross. 'I'm going to be having my hands full with the first of my fourteen children!'

'Be a good girl and I'll cut it to six.' He gave her a pat on the shoulder and wandered off to his den, a small room at the back of the house, too small to have been included in the estate agent's list.

Hester prepared lunch and then went upstairs to look in her wardrobe. The things she'd hauled out yesterday were bound to need pressing, and she hadn't much choice anyway, not unless a pair of slacks and a cotton shirt would do—she had plenty of those.

'There's quite a nice boutique in Esher, I passed it on my way back this morning.' Once again Demetrios was standing behind her, peering over her shoulder at the row of hangers, and she hadn't heard a sound—the sound of his voice startled her and she swung round.

'Must you creep everywhere?' she scowled ferociously. 'It's very upsetting.'

'So are the contents of your wardrobe.' He reached over her shoulder and flicked through the hangers. 'Why on earth haven't you bought yourself some new clothes? The only thing you've bought since we've been married is that black evening thing. Come on, we've got an hour to spare before lunch. Let's get you something decent to wear this afternoon.'

Hester had been going to say 'no', but something stopped her—possibly the knowledge that she really hadn't anything suitable, not for a confrontation with Vilma and Athene, who would be dolled up to the nines. On the other hand, she was reluctant to spend any of the money she had in the bank. She might need that—there would be a bedsit to find and the landlady would expect rent in advance—and until she could contact Crispin, start to work and work for a month, she'd have no salary. Of course, she could always ask Crispin for an advance, but she dismissed that thought almost as soon as it entered her head. Crispin knew she had married a rich man and his eyebrows would vanish over the top of his head if she appeared to be poverty-stricken.

She could always go back to Poplar, though, it wouldn't cost her anything much to live in the flat with Mia, but she couldn't ask Mia for money. Every penny her foster-sister could save was put towards her plane fare to Switzerland. This was no time for pride.

'As long as you're paying,' she answered brightly, 'I'll buy everything in the boutique that fits me. Let's go. It's only a cold lunch, so it won't spoil.'

Demetrios paid for her purchases, and she gulped at

the amount while maintaining a sophisticated appearance.

'Cleaned you out, darling,' she murmured as he fiddled with something small in one pocket of his wallet. 'What's that?'

'A new calculator.' He flipped back the flap that covered the pocket and she could see the digital display. 'Very useful things, these—small enough to keep in your pocket but they keep me up to date with the money in the various accounts.'

'Men and their toys!' she sniffed. 'I'd have thought an accountant could do little sums like that in his head!' She tripped past him and out on to the pavement, carrying some of the bags and boxes and leaving him to bring the rest.

'You expect a lot.' Demetrios tossed the parcels into the back of the car, opened the door for her and then slid behind the wheel. 'Even I can't keep track of eight different accounts—therefore the calculator. It has a better memory than I have.'

'I wonder you admit it,' Hester marvelled, then peeped inside the bag which she had clung to jealously. 'Did you like it—the dress, I mean?'

'Mmm,' he flicked her a wicked look. 'If it hadn't been for the saleswoman I'd have made love to you on the spot.' He watched the road, swerving to avoid oncoming traffic, and when he next spoke, all the laughter had gone from his voice and he was deeply serious. 'What's the matter, Hester? You've been on edge all morning. Are you bothered about meeting your mother?'

Hester shrugged. 'Could be.'

'But why? You've met her before, twice, I think. There was the time in the hotel after the wedding and then when she came down here. . . .'

'You've been having me watched!' Hester exclaimed. 'Well, of all the underhanded things to do!'

'You weren't being watched,' he laughed at her stupidity. 'There's never been any need to watch you, my darling—you lose your temper and everything spills out. You told me yourself, remember? And you hoped I'd missed it, but I don't miss much, and certainly not something as blatant as that. You said Vilma noticed the resemblance between Katy and Athene although it was only from a photograph in our sitting room, and even if you hadn't mentioned the sitting-room, I'd have known anyway. That's the only photograph there is of Katy. After the kidnap attempt, I had all photographs of her destroyed—that way, she was just another little girl, she couldn't be picked out from among half a dozen others.'

'Elementary, my dear Watson!' Hester subsided in her seat.

'Then let's take it one elementary step further. What did Vilma want—money?'

'Work it out for yourself.' Her eyes glinted with a spark of triumph. 'She knows I don't have any. As a matter of fact, she said I was like her—another Greek wife, housed, fed, clothed and occasionally sprinkled all over with diamonds, but no money.'

Demetrios took one hand off the steering wheel, felt in his pocket among the loose change and extracted a fifty-pence piece. 'Buy yourself some sweets,' he said as he tossed it in her lap.

Hester's fingers closed over the coin, it was warm from his pocket and she thought she'd keep it for ever. Many girls would have been insulted, but not her. Apart from the black dress and the clothes he had just bought her, it was the only thing Demetrios had given her—she didn't count the pearls, he hadn't given her those—he'd decorated her with them with as little thought as he would have given to hanging a glass bauble on a Christmas tree.

Love was such a funny thing—one minute it was love and the next, utter misery. Loving him, being loved by him, was heaven—it was the high of her life, but one couldn't stay up on the peaks for ever and the higher she went, the further she had to fall and the deeper the pit into which she fell.

Slowly she relaxed, sinking back into the rich leather upholstery. This afternoon would tell. If Demetrios loved her he would trust her, but until then, she would make life good for both of them.

'Sorry,' she muttered. 'But it's like you said, I'm not looking forward to this afternoon. Couldn't I just stay here? You don't need me when you meet Vilma.'

'And miss the chance of showing off my wife in all her new finery? I wouldn't dream of it.' He reached out a hand and clasped her cold fingers comfortingly. 'Don't worry so much, my sweet. Trust me instead. I'm telling you, everything will be all right.'

'Will it?' she enquired bleakly. 'I love you. I didn't want to, not like this—it robs me—makes me dependent. . . .'

'And what's wrong with that?' His hand touched hers again. 'Get yourself together, my sweet, otherwise I shall have to pull the car off the road and we'll provide a fine sight for any passers-by to gawp at.'

Hester's depression lifted as she pictured them, clinging to each other, rather abandoned, and all in the enormous dignity of the Rolls. She giggled. 'I couldn't think of anything I'd like better!'

'You'll wait till we get home,' he told her sternly.

Hester carefully adjusted the tilt of her cream straw boater and pirouetted so that the pleated skirt of her

her apple green silk shirtwaister swung about her slender legs. 'Nice?' she queried of her husband, who was lying lazily on the bed and watching her every move. Somehow it seemed no longer improper to dress in front of him, and in any case, she had had no option. He had been sprawled there when she had come from the bath with only a towelling robe over her bra and panties and he had refused to move.

'Mmm,' his dark eyes flickered over her appreciatively. 'Come here,' and he held out a lazy hand.

'Not on your life!' she laughed softly. 'I've put a lot of work into looking like this and you'll spoil it. You'll rumple me up and eat my lipstick.'

'Hardhearted woman,' he growled, 'and after I bought you the finery!'

'Not all of it.' Hester contemplated her slender legs and admired the sheen of pure silk stockings and the way her pale, high-heeled shoes flattered her feet. 'Shoes, bag and gloves—left-overs from my wedding outfit—a shame to waste them.' She touched the filmy lace that decorated the collar and tight cuffs of the dress. 'They match this and the hat. It saved a lot of money.'

'Thrift—that's what I like.' Demetrios levered himself up from the bed and reached for the clothes brush to flick away a piece of lint from his trousers. 'Well, if you won't, you won't. Come on, let's get it over. We'll find somewhere quiet to have dinner on the way home.'

The hotel suite was as bland and lacking in personality as ever, and Hester wrinkled her nose. 'I'm so glad we don't live here, it would be like living in the middle of a caramel pudding. Thank you for the house, Demetrios.'

'So it is.' His eyes sparkled at her. 'Nearly tasteless and goes with everything—I hadn't noticed it before. Shall I order tea now or would you wait till our visitors arrive?'

'We'll wait,' she giggled. 'Just imagine what it would be like trying to say "good afternoon" through a mouthful of cucumber sandwich! It *will* be cucumber, won't it?'

'I imagine so, and with the choice of Indian, China or Earl Grey tea.'

'Very Edwardian, just like *The Importance of Being Earnest*.' She chuckled. 'We'll have Earl Grey and keep everything in period.'

'Mmm.' Demetrios crossed the room to the service phone. 'I'll order now and tell them to send it up when Vilma arrives.'

Hester sat hard on the impulse to tell him to order for four—it wasn't necessary, her gaiety was a cover-up for extreme nervousness because she knew that, of course, Athene would come with Vilma—what good was a story without the supporting evidence? And an extra cup and saucer could readily be obtained.

The door to the suite opened just before he put down the phone and she heard his, 'Now,' before she looked up. Vilma swanned in without even a knock, looking beautiful as ever but in some way brittle and preserved, like a blown and varnished eggshell—weightless and delicate. Athene followed her, but today the Greek woman was not out to catch the eye. Her silver-grey dress was a perfect foil for Vilma's blue, it looked almost dim, and Hester knew now what Vilma had meant when she said that Athene preferred to stage-manage.

The last time they had all been together in this suite, Athene had been out of character—sparkly and with a desire to make an impact. That had been bad enough, but today, softly grey and in the background, she was quiet, almost withdrawn. But the iron was showing through; Athene was much more dangerous like this. Hester met the implacable gaze of dark, Byzantine eyes, and it was all she could do to hold her own steady in the face of such hostility.

Fortunately, the waiter practically followed the visitors in and in the general hoo-ha of arranging everything just where she could manage it easily, Hester had time to cool herself down to an outward appearance of pleasant anticipation of a cup of tea. She poured while the weather, politics, the depression and its effect on business and the latest musical were discussed, complimenting herself on putting up quite a good show, considering she knew very little about any of them but the weather—and then Demetrios spoiled it all.

'What did you want to see me about, Vilma?' He evidently wasn't going to waste time on idle chat.

Vilma stopped saying what she thought about the musical's success and looked across at him, her eyes like two blue china beads, round, hard and utterly lacking in expression. 'You don't show much finesse, Demos, but I suppose it *would* be better to get it over.' She picked up a tiny, triangular sandwich, put it on her plate and then ignored it while she set her cup and saucer down on the wide arm of her chair—and then quietly, in an emotionless voice, she told her story, word for word as she had told it to Hester.

Hester recognised each well-rehearsed phrase and her heart sank. It was all right for her, she'd heard it before and she knew it wasn't the truth, but if she had been a completely dispassionate listener, simply hearing it for the first time, she would find it most convincing, and Demetrios *was* hearing it for the first time!

He sat there in his chair, completely silent, his eyes never leaving Vilma, giving her his whole attention until she'd finished, and then he looked at Hester. She returned his gaze calmly, searching his eyes for something—and then it was there. A bubble of happiness swam up into her throat and burst, swamping her with relief so that she nearly cried for the glory of it. He hadn't said a word—he didn't have to! That one long look was enough, it said more than any words could ever have conveyed, and it was at that moment that Athene broke the silence, in Greek, fast and fierce like a volcano spewing out lava. It went on for nearly half a minute until, surprisingly, Vilma interrupted the flow.

'Do be quiet, Athene!' Her voice was cold and cutting like a well sharpened knife. 'I can only guess what you're saying, but you're wasting your breath. Can't you see that? Hester could have stolen the Crown Jewels and Demos wouldn't give a damn—she could have planned to rob the Bank of England and he'd probably help her do it.' Her voice rose a little and the knife cut more savagely. 'Look at them, Athene! Don't you see what you want is out of reach? Demos is besotted with her. For God's sake, show a little dignity! It was a good try, but you've lost and so have I. Bury your dreams and settle for second best, as all of us have to do at one time or another. There are some things even your money won't buy!'

Dark, Byzantine eyes slid over Demetrios, lingering briefly, and then passed on to Hester, and she shrank from the venom in their depths. Involuntarily, her hand went out to her husband and was taken in a firm, warm grip that comforted her. She closed her eyes and when she opened them Athene was gone, a dark-eyed, grey little ghost who would haunt her no more.

Demetrios broke the rather uncomfortable silence which had fallen. 'And now, Vilma, shall we finish with fairy tales? How much do you want, and why?'

'How much?' Vilma shrugged as she took a sip of tea and Hester looked at her mother with a new respect. That brittle, well-preserved look wasn't that of an eggshell—that was only what it looked like. It was bullet-proof steel; nothing, but nothing would make an impression on it. Vilma would be dignified, even in defeat. 'Ten thousand,' she shrugged again gracefully. 'Gambling debts, Demos. You know how Sandros is about things like that, I can have what I like as long as I've got something to show for it. I suppose I should have put them down on that list I gave you, but,' another shrug, 'you've always disapproved of me. . . .'

'On the contrary,' Demetrios gave her a long, speculative look, 'I don't disapprove of you at all, as a wife for my uncle, that is. In fact, in my opinion, he couldn't have married anyone better suited to be his wife. You're selfish and self-centred, but that only serves to keep you faithful to him—you wouldn't cheat on him with another man, you'd stand to lose too much and you know it, and cheating on Uncle Sandros like that is about the only way you could really hurt him.' He reached into his pocket and drew out the leather case which contianed his cheque book and calculator. 'Your story wasn't nice, but I don't give you all the credit for it. I've never before known you to work anything out in such detail, or even plan that far ahead. You generally act on impulse and then rely on your femininity and a sob story to get you out of trouble.'

Vilma gave him a wry smile. 'But it was a good try, wasn't it? And I was going to be well paid for it if it came off.' Her eyes flicked to Hester. 'I told you I was a compulsive gambler, and when we'd worked out the scheme, all the details, it looked like a winner. Thanks,' as she took the cheque Demetrios had written and examined it. 'I'll give you no more trouble, either of you.'

'No, I don't think you will.' Demetrios' smile wasn't kind. 'I don't forgive or forget this sort of thing easily, not when it means unhappiness for my wife. Remember that, if you're ever tempted again—and also remember that your chance of finding another husband as rich as Sandros grows less every day. I think you should be looking to the future, because with luck, you stand a good chance of being a rich widow in ten to twenty years' time and it would be a pity to spoil that promising future. Uncle Sandros has that villa up on the Halkidiki peninsula, he likes it there, far better than living in London or Athens—he likes to take his boat and do a bit of fishing. I think that's where you should go, and settle down to a peaceful life. He thinks the world of you and he won't care a bit if you get fat or your hair goes white. I shall call on you there in October and I hope I will find you both very happy and contented.'

'You weren't very kind.' Vilma had gone, after finishing her tea, and Hester was once more alone with her husband. 'Vilma told me you could be cruel, something to do with the Turkish blood in you—but to practically banish her and then to suggest she might get fat—that was definitely a blow beneath the belt! Is your uncle retiring?'

'Yes,' Demetrios scowled. 'He's tired of boardroom

meetings—of waving the big stick—of, as he says, fronting the company. He says it's time I did my own job instead of leaving it to an old, tired man. He wants to go fishing.'

'Fronting the company?' Hester was mystified.

'Mmm.' Demetrios came to sit on the arm of her chair, lifted the cream boater from her head and skimmed it across to fall on the teapot. 'He's been doing it since my father died; in those days, he looked so much better at the job than I did—a big bull of a man, whereas I was a callow youth. I didn't have the right appearance, I didn't know enough and I was a bit of a playboy. I'm afraid it will mean a bit more travelling, will you mind that?'

'N-no——' Hester hesitated. 'I don't think I'll mind anything now. I wanted you to love me, but I also wanted you to trust me. We started off on the wrong foot, remember, and I thought you didn't—trust me, I mean, but now I know you do. You told me this afternoon without words.'

'You're learning, my darling.' He pulled her closer and one hand stroked her rich hair. 'Words are clumsy things at best except in the hands of a poet, and I'm no poet, I can only quote, and sometimes I don't get that right. "Shall I compare thee to a summer's day, Thou art more lovely and more temperate", with the accent on "temper" of course.'

'Ta very much!' she snorted. 'But you do understand, don't you? You said I hadn't to be like that Nemesis woman. We didn't do much Greek mythology in the school I went to, so I looked her up. She was always after vengeance and retribution but I didn't feel that way about Vilma. I wasn't being vengeful when I asked for that money. If it hadn't been for Flo, I'd never have bothered with her at all—she means nothing to me.'

'Flo?'

'Mmm.' She raised her head to look at him. 'My foster-mother. She's very ill, and Mia—that's my foster-sister—she and I were at our wits' end. Mia'd found this doctor with a clinic in Switzerland. . . .' Quietly, Hester went on with the sad little story. 'So you see,' she finished, 'there wasn't any revenge about it, we just needed the money.' Her lips curved in a reminiscent smile. 'I wanted to ask for twenty-five thousand, that would have given Flo fifty weeks, but Mia said I was pushing it, so we settled on twenty thousand. And don't think badly of Mia, she didn't like it much. It was all my idea.'

'Didn't I tell you words aren't necessary.' Demetrios put his arm about her shoulders and tightened it into a hug while he dropped a kiss on the top of her head. 'Within twenty minutes of meeting you, I knew you had a good reason for wanting so much money, and I also knew that one day you'd tell me what it was—the day you decided to trust me.'

'The day *you* decided to trust *me*!' she corrected.

'And do you think I'd have handed over the care of my daughter to a woman I didn't trust?' He raised an eyebrow. 'You're exceptionally dim about some things, my sweet. Now, let me see if I get the same answer this time,' and he reached for the calculator and started punching the buttons.

'Men and their toys!' Hester scoffed. 'There's nothing that thing can do that I can't, given a pencil, a piece of paper and time.'

'You think not?' Demetrios' eyes gleamed at her while his mouth curved in an aggravating smile. 'How long have we been married? Ten weeks, isn't it? My calculator says you're pregnant.'

'Bosh!' she retorted. 'There must be something

wrong with it, perhaps its little silicon chip's been chipped, or you could have been pressing the wrong buttons. If I was, I'd know, although I admit I'm not genned up on that sort of thing.' She looked up at him pertly. 'I suppose you are?

'That's a blow beneath the belt,' he reproved her. 'I admit only to knowing far more now than when I was a young man in Cyprus, but *not* from any personal experience.'

Hester ignored him; her mind had gone off on to another tack. 'Vilma said you were a besotted husband,' she made the remark in a dreamy voice. 'I rather like that idea.'

'But I don't like the word.' He put his arm about her waist and heaved her to her feet. She retrieved her hat from the teapot and together they went out to the lift where, once inside and the door closed on them, he imprisoned her with a hand on either shoulder.

'Besotted isn't a nice word when applied to me. It makes a man sound like mush.' His mouth found hers and reduced her to a willing pulp. 'Now it's all right for you to be mushy about me,' he told her when he raised his head. 'That's just as it should be. For instance. . . .'

'Give me a "for instance",' she murmured softly.

The lift stopped with a bump, the door slid open and he shook his head ruefully. 'Not now, there may be somebody watching, we'll wait till we get home.'

Because Katy wasn't at home, there was no need for such an early breakfast, and Hester turned over lazily at half past eight to find Demetrios placing a cup of tea on the bedside table. Her eyes slid over him with pleasure—good to look at, and all hers—she closed her eyes again tightly with joy.

'Don't pretend.' He leaned over and kissed her. 'I

know you're awake. Drink your tea while I deal with the post. Hmm,' he riffled through the small sheaf of envelopes. 'Mostly circulars—there's one for you, though.'

'One for me?' She sat up in bed instantly and held out her hand. Only one person would be writing to her here—Mia, and for Mia to have sent her a letter meant news of Flo. The letter felt cold and ominous when he put it in her hand and she raised apprehensive eyes to him.

'Open it for me and read it, please,' she muttered over the sick feeling in her stomach. 'It'll be from Mia, about Flo. Oh, I *knew* I shouldn't have gone out yesterday, she must have been phoning all afternoon. . . .'

'Stop getting hysterical!' His sharp tone cut through her babblings and she waited silently while he slit the envelope, read the letter and the enclosure which was typed on thick white paper. Finally he pushed both into her hands. 'See for yourself,' he advised. 'To me it sounds promising.'

The phrases sprang out at her from the typed sheet. 'No further deterioration'—'Cautious hope'—'optimism'—and the room swam around her as she sighed with relief and started reading Mia's covering note while Demetrios dealt with the remainder of the mail, among which was a small, thickly padded envelope. He opened it and put a cottonwool wrapped package in her lap. She raised her eyes from Mia's hasty scrawl.

'What's this?' she enquired.

Quietly he took the letters from her and putting a finger under her chin, tilted her face up. 'Ten weeks ago, outside your bedsitter, we both of us behaved badly. Me, because I was jealous and you because you were hurt. I want to wipe out that memory and this is the only way I could do it. Will you be equally generous, Hester?'

She unwrapped the cotton wool and looked down at her leaves, repaired and re-plated—as good as new, and this time the tears rose to her eyes and she let them fall, to roll down her cheeks.

'Who's being generous?' she growled. 'I was a perfect pig.' She lifted a hand and wiped her wet face with the back of it. 'Please keep loving me, darling,' she whispered, 'don't ever stop.'

'I couldn't if I wanted to.' There was no laughter in his eyes, they were dark and serious. 'It's a life sentence, my love. I'll do it until the day I die.'

Hester's reply was never uttered; with a convulsive gasp, she sprang out of bed and grabbed for her gown. 'I think your damn calculator could be right after all!' she gasped as she fled to the bathroom and shut the door firmly on Demetrios' whoop of triumphant laughter.

Share the joys and sorrows of real-life love with
Harlequin American Romance!™

GET THIS BOOK FREE as your introduction to Harlequin American Romance — an exciting series of romance novels written especially for the American woman of today.

Mail to:
Harlequin Reader Service

In the U.S.
2504 West Southern Ave.
Tempe, AZ 85282

In Canada
P.O. Box 2800, Postal Station A
5170 Yonge St., Willowdale, Ont. M2N 6J3

YES! I want to be one of the first to discover
Harlequin American Romance. Send me FREE and without obligation *Twice in a Lifetime*. If you do not hear from me after I have examined my FREE book, please send me the 4 new **Harlequin American Romances** each month as soon as they come off the presses. I understand that I will be billed only $2.25 for each book (total $9.00). There are no shipping or handling charges. There is no minimum number of books that I have to purchase. In fact, I may cancel this arrangement at any time. *Twice in a Lifetime* is mine to keep as a FREE gift, even if I do not buy any additional books.   154 BPA NAZJ

Name _____ (please print)

Address _____ Apt. no.

City _____ State/Prov. _____ Zip/Postal Code

Signature (If under 18, parent or guardian must sign.)

This offer is limited to one order per household and not valid to current Harlequin American Romance subscribers. We reserve the right to exercise discretion in granting membership. If price changes are necessary, you will be notified.

AMR-SUB-1